THE CHILD WAS GROWING EVEN AS SHE LOOKED AT IT.

It twisted and contorted, whining with the effort it was making. Legs and arms lengthened before her eyes. The torso expanded. Facial features began to crinkle and develop definition. And with each new spurt of growth it threw off a brilliant flash of light.

It was impossible. She stood there, halfway through the doorway, trying to make some sense out of what she was witnessing. She held the back of her right hand against her open mouth and seemed suddenly unable to close her jaws, just as she was unable to tear her gaze away from the thing on the floor of her living room.

It was bigger now, much bigger. In the poor light she couldn't make out many details, and each flash of light left her half-blinded. The infant was long gone now. In its place a grown man lay twisting and turning on the hardwood floor . . .

And he had Scott's face.

Also by Alan Dean Foster

KRULL

and published by Corgi Books

STARMAN

Alan Dean Foster

from the screenplay by
Ray Gideon, Bruce Evans, and Dean Riesner

CORGI BOOKS

STARMAN

A CORGI BOOK 0 552 12688 8

First publication in Great Britain

PRINTING HISTORY

Corgi edition published 1985

This book is set in 10pt Baskerville

Corgi Books are published by Transworld Publishers Ltd.,
Century House, 61-63 Uxbridge Road, Ealing, London W5 5SA,
in Australia by Transworld Publishers (Aust.) Pty. Ltd.,
26 Harley Crescent, Condell Park, NSW 2200, and in
New Zealand by Transworld Publishers (N.Z.) Ltd.,
Cnr. Moselle and Waipareira Avenue, Henderson, Auckland.

Printed and bound in Great Britain by
Cox & Wyman Ltd, Reading

For Peter Branham –
Who's better than he thinks

One

Nobody saw the ship.

It came in quietly on little hypergravitic cat feet and didn't steal silently away. Instead, it assumed an orbit some sixty thousand kilometers out from the surface of the beautiful blue-and-white planet. No notice was taken of it by the inhabitants of the planet below because the crew of the ship did not wish to be noticed. They maintained their anonymity by the simple expedient of diverting any questing impulses around themselves. Devices within the ship were capable of bending gravity waves. Diverting radar was far simpler.

In a special chamber deep within the bowels of the great ship was an Object. They had found the Object drifting forlornly through interstellar space, going nowhere at a ridiculously slow pace. Within its hard metal body the lonely traveler contained primitive visual and aural encodings. It didn't take the crew long to break down the codes into thousands of bits of comprehensible information. What the translation of those kilobytes of random ramblings said was, more or less, 'Hi.' In addition to the greetings there were directions, of a sort.

There was discussion and argument, the outcome of which was a decision to go and see what the builders of the traveler might be about. There was conversation and consultation across parsecs, the result of which was that the ship changed course.

Having completed the journey the ship hovered now above the traveler's world of origin. From within the crew observed silently, recording and monitoring, taking readings and making measurements. This went on for some time. But no matter how sophisticated the instrumentation, there are some things that cannot be learned from a distance of sixty thousand kilometers. Study from a distance must ultimately give way to intimate examination.

There was never any doubt which of them would take the critical, necessary next step. He was an exceptional individual even among his own kind (we will call him a 'he' for the sake of biological expediency). Despite the danger inherent in visiting any primitive world of unknown hazards and potential, his fellow crew-members envied him. There were no protests, however. None argued to go in his stead. The people who crewed the great ship had long since outgrown such absurdities as envy. Each of them knew full well that the one selected to make the drop was by far the best qualified of any of them to do so.

The explorer entered his tiny drop vessel without fanfare. There were no crowds of well-wishers standing by to see him off, and none needed. The rest of the crew was busy attending to their respective tasks. If asked to explain their attitude they would have replied that moments spent on frivolity are moments lost to the triumph of entropy. That was the real enemy, not any rambunctious primitives inhabiting the world below.

Not that they didn't feel concern for him. Even a brief survey of a backward world entailed certain risks. So there were silent expressions of concern for the explorer's safety as the hatch opened in the flank of the great ship and the little research craft eased out into space. The crew know one another well. They were more than a family, and the explorer was one of them. The sooner his task was completed and he was safely back among them, the easier all would rest.

Despite this anxiety they were all anxious to learn the results of the forthcoming survey. They were hopeful as well as nervous. In the vast loneliness of the universe, intelligence was a rare and precious commodity. If the

8

explorer's survey proved fruitful it would mean that the galaxy would become a little less empty.

Part of the danger to the explorer stemmed from the small size of his vessel. It was designed to travel hither and yon, into difficult to reach places, while attracting a minimum of attention. Because of its smallness it did not have room for the instrumentation that could deflect curious varieties of energy around itself. It would be open to detection from the surface.

Both the explorer and the crew hoped this would not make any difference in his mission. They had reason to be hopeful. The size of the drop craft would make it hard to notice, and the design of the interstellar traveler whose message they had deciphered suggested that the technology of its makers was still quite primitive.

Carmichael leaned back in the chair, turned the magazine sideways to let the centerfold tumble free, and studied the resultant anatomical schematic with considerable interest. His powers of concentration were admirable and he missed nothing. Despite this he felt compelled to review the glossy display several times before refolding it back into the parent magazine. With a sigh he moved on to an article by William F. Buckley, Jr, trying but failing to muster as much enthusiasm for it as he had for the previous pages.

The readout nearby which indicated climatological conditions outside informed him that the temperature was eighty-four and the humidity ridiculously high. Around him it was pleasantly cool. He knew that the air conditioning was there more for the benefit of the machinery he monitored than for himself, but he didn't mind.

Around him, tons of intricately woven metal formed a gigantic dish that scanned the sky around the clock. The dish's job was to search for electronic anomalies. It had been doing its job patiently and without much success for many years now. Carmichael recognized the occasional bleep or squirp that issued from a speaker in front of him.

9

No surprises. They didn't interrupt his reading. It was a good job for a man who liked to read.

And he was good at it. It required a special kind of patience to be able to sit alone in the room perusing centerfold after centerfold without going over the edge and breaking up the furniture.

A telltale buzzed, drawing the attention of one eye to a video monitor set among dozens of others in the wall of instruments. Carmichael frowned to himself, set the acerbic conservative's opinions aside, and sat up straight in his chair. He was concentrating on the one screen to the exclusion of everything else in the room.

Still there – the anomaly. He got out of the chair and began fine-tuning controls. The anomaly would not go away. If anything, it loomed larger the longer he worked on it. Now not only Buckley but his pneumatic predecessor as well were forgotten. Carmichael felt a sensation not normally attendant upon his job: excitement.

Nearby, a computer printer began machine-gunning information onto paper. He yanked it out of the printer as soon as the hard copy was completed. There it was, in full color. Proof of an impossibility. Scientifically speaking, his ass was covered.

He reached for the special phone.

Matthews and Ford watched the line of little yellow lights come to life on the screen in front of them. The screen was transparent and you could see through it, past the yellow dots and the bright green and red lines the yellow one was crossing. The two men were watching the screen with the intensity of a couple of fifteen years olds at the local video arcade who were down to their last quarter. There were significant differences, however. The screen they were watching cost millions to operate, and the movement of the yellow lights was beyond their control. They were spectators instead of participants.

'This is crazy.' Matthews spoke without turning away from the screen. The growing line of yellow lights had him mesmerized.

'It's right where Arcebio said it would be.'

'Crazy.' Two more dots came to yellow life, extending the line still further. If the line kept growing it would soon intersect the irregular red line on the left-hand side of the screen. That would be very significant, because the red line indicated the coastline of the state of Washington.

Other men and women glanced over from their positions in front of smaller, console-mounted screens. They badly wanted to join Matthews and Ford but could not leave their own posts. A third figure who was not constrained by such considerations joined the first two in eyeing the screen. He was short, old, and didn't have much hair left. Instead of hair, an aura of power clung to him.

'What do you think, gentlemen?' he finally asked Matthews and Ford. 'Is she Soviet?'

Ford considered. 'Possible. North Pacific origin, high-level atmospheric entry, radical angle of descent, and it's up there all by its lonesome. Maybe they're probing us with a dud to see if they can slip one through.'

'ICBM?'

Matthews shook his head. 'That's what's crazy, sir. It's moving much too slowly. I don't figure it at all. What's more, it appears to vary its speed.'

'What about a variable-orbit reconnaissance satellite?'

'If so, it's full of stuff we've never heard of. I've never seen anything behave like this before. Weird.'

'I don't need weird. I need what it is.'

'No can say, sir,' Ford told him.

'But it's definitely not ours?'

Both men shook their heads. 'Not unless some agency's running one hell of a clever test,' Ford added.

'No, it's no test,' said their superior. He watched the screen in silence. Another yellow light appeared, crossing the red coastline. That was enough. He turned, crossed to a desk, and picked up a telephone. He didn't have to dial the number he wanted. The phone had no dial. But everyone in the room watched him anyway. No one spoke.

* * *

11

'Beautiful night, George.' The general was in an ebullient mood and not at all adverse to letting his fellow concert-goers know it.

George Fox, the director of the National Security Agency, smiled back at his friend, took a sip of his martini, and gazed out across the Potomac. There were only five minutes of intermission remaining. He was going to have to hurry the martini if he wanted to finish it. That was a shame, because he was enjoying the relaxed evening. For a change, the world tonight was a relatively peaceful place. The Mozart had soothed him and he was looking forward to the stimulating Janaček to come.

He could simply dispose of the remainder of his drink, but that would be painful. He hated waste. It was one reason why he'd risen as high within the government as he had.

'Yes, it is pretty out,' he agreed. 'How're the kids?'

The general shrugged. 'Same. I'm trying to wean Debbie away from M-TV. She's sixteen.'

The naval flag officer who formed the third member of the triumvirate commiserated with his colleague. 'That's going to be tough. You know, for the price of one guided-missile frigate we could beam the stuff to every household in Russia. End the cold war inside a month.'

'Not a bad idea,' the general admitted. 'Think they'd accept Michael Jackson as the new tsar?' Both men laughed quietly. Fox did not. He didn't laugh much.

The out-of-breath lieutenant finally spotted them standing on the outside promenade, turned toward them. He was trying to move quickly through the crowd without attracting attention.

'Mister Director?'

Fox turned to the newcomer. He betrayed only the slightest hint of the irritation he felt. He had this sinking feeling he wasn't going to be allowed to enjoy the rest of the concert.

'Yes?' The lieutenant handed him a manila envelope. Fox slipped the seal and studied the message contained

12

within. As was the nature of such communiqués it was brief, to the point, and full of implications. He read it over a second time before slipping it back into the envelope. The two senior military officers standing nearby studiously diverted their attention elsewhere.

The general did his best to sound casual. 'Something important, George?'

Fox replied with a thin smile. 'I don't think so, but you know how these things are. Somebody else does, and so I'm stuck with soothing frazzled nerves. It comes with the territory. Let me know how the rest of the concert went, will you?'

The naval officer nodded sympathetically. 'Sure, George.'

Both men watched as their companion turned and walked rapidly toward the nearest stairway.

'What do you suppose that was all about?' the general wondered aloud.

His colleague shrugged. 'Like he said, it's probably the usual much ado about nothing.'

'Yeah.' The general was silent a moment, then added, 'I wouldn't have his job for all the diamonds in South Africa.'

The corridor was spotlessly clean and well lit by numerous overhead fluorescents. Doors were identified only by numbers. There were no windows. Fox and his assistant walked briskly, ignoring the occasional passing pedestrian.

'Sounds like Russian space-garbage to me, Brayton. If it was an accidental launching we'd have heard from them pronto, and if it was deliberate we'd know by now. Our sources aren't that bad. So it's got to be their junk.'

'The Molink people say no.' Brayton was thoughtful, precise, and not particularly imaginative. Fox found him very useful.

'What does the Kremlin say about it?'

'*Naz drovya* and how's the weather out your way? They don't know from nothin'.'

Fox grunted. 'If it is theirs they might have plenty of

13

reasons for not wanting to claim it. If the Molink people still say it ain't and if it's still behaving as erratically as it was when we first picked it up, it could still qualify as some new kind of surveillance job. Or it might be another worn-out military satellite with its reactor intact, like the one that came apart over Canada a few years back. If either case is true, our Soviet friends will declare their innocence until we can slap some hard evidence in their faces.'

They reached the end of the corridor and pushed through the door at the far end. Beyond lay an auditorium alive with teletypes, oversized video screens, monitoring consoles and mildly frantic attendant personnel. Brayton and Fox headed straight for a center console around which several NSA people were clustered. One of the group noticed their approach and informed the other of the director's presence.

'What've we got?' Fox asked curtly.

'Bunch of F-16s from McCord picked it up over the mountains, sir,' the man informed him. 'It didn't respond to multiple hailings. They tried calling it on all the standard frequencies. No response. Went right over the Trident sub base at Bremerton and at that point the local brass went through the roof. A couple of the fighters made a pass at it without getting a look-see – it was going too fast – but they claim they got a hit.'

'They would. Independent confirmation?'

'No apparent damage, so nobody knows yet if the pilots were lucky or just guessing, but whatever the reason, we've got another change of course.'

Fox's eyebrows rose. Next to him Brayton mumbled, 'Space-garbage doesn't change course once it hits lower atmosphere.' His boss ignored him.

The operative turned back to the console, studied the constantly changing readouts. 'Got a new estimated point of impact.' He looked up, gestured toward a map of the United States outlined in glowing colors on the big screen that dominated one wall of the auditorium. 'Northern Wisconsin someplace.'

'Crap,' Fox muttered, staring at the electronic map. 'If it lands in one of those big lakes up there we'll never find it.' He said almost off-handedly to Brayton, 'Get ahold of Mark Shermin.'

The image on the television screen in the apartment living room was oversized, as was the player dribbling the basketball. Crowd noises spilled out of the stereo speakers and filled the room. The play-by-play announcer was barely audible above the roar of the fans:

'. . . and the score is New Jersey one-oh-one, the Washington Bullets one hundred. If Ruland can hit these two free throws that'll be five in a row at home for the Bullets!'

There was nothing remarkable about the appearance of the man who walked into the living room. What marked him as unusual was not visible. He had a mind of exceptional depth and was particularly noted for an ability to assimilate reams of seemingly unconnected facts and reduce them to one or two simple, obvious conclusions that everyone else wondered why they hadn't seen in the first place.

Right now that mind was wondering whether or not Jeff Ruland, one of the better free-throw shooters in the NBA for a big man, was going to crack under the pressure of having to make a pair of potentially game-winning charity tosses.

Mark Shermin used his right forearm to sweep his desk clear of debris. He had to do it that way because both hands were full: one with a sloppy sandwich on old french bread and the other with a bottle of beer. The beer was Hinano Export. He got an occasional case from a friend whose job it was to fly blackbirds over the French National atomic-testing site at Muroroa Atoll in the South Pacific.

As he sat down the swept-away papers went flying. Some of them were marked in bold stenciled letters SECRET and CONFIDENTIAL. Shermin's casual treatment of them made sense if one realized that only a few people in the world could make up or down of their contents. His cleaning lady wasn't among that small elite.

His attention was focused on the screen as he took a mouthful of sandwich and a swig of beer. Meat sauce trickled down his chin. He wiped it away with the back of one hand.

Ruland made the first free throw, tying the score. The crowd went wild. When he missed the second, thereby sending the game into overtime, a collective groan issued from the speaker. Shermin added his own opinion and started in seriously on the sandwich.

The damnphone rang. Always to Shermin it was the damnphone; never the damn phone. It continued to ring, insistent, demanding, like an electronic mistress. Eyes still locked on the TV he growled softly and picked up the receiver.

'Call back in twenty minutes, I'm . . .'

Whoever was on the other end managed to slip a word in before Shermin could break the connection. He made a face, reached for the remote control and muted the sound of the TV. Not many callers could make him do that. Not with the Bullets heading into overtime.

'Yes sir? What? Sure, no problem. No, I was just watching the Bullets' game. Overtime. Yeah, I'm sorry too. Chequamegon Bay? Where the hell's that, up near Baltimore? Wisconsin?' He sighed, set the sandwich aside. 'Yes sir, whatever you say, sir.'

He hung up, sat thinking for a long moment. Then he turned the sound back up. Whatever it was could wait a few minutes longer. It couldn't possibly be as important as the outcome of the game.

The cabin was small and contemporary, woodsy without being primitive, cozy but not cramped. It fit the young woman in her twenties who was sitting in the middle of the living-room floor. Her name was Jenny Hayden and she was equally engrossed in the home movies unspooling on the screen in front of her and the bottle of wine she was

16

drinking. The bottle was nearly empty and Jenny Hayden was more than full. But she kept watching and she kept drinking because she didn't know how to stop doing either.

The picture on the screen was grainy but the bay outside the cabin was easily recognizable. The camera was watching a man only slightly older than Jenny herself. He was paddling toward the camera in a canoe, mouthing amiable inanities as he approached.

Suddenly he stood up, turned his back toward the camera, pulled down his pants, and bent over. This complex maneuver proving too much for his sense of balance, if not his sense of humor, he promptly went overboard, waving his arms wildly as he went into the lake.

The camera searched the empty surface when without warning a face erupted in front of it and spat a mouthful of water straight into the lens. This was followed by a cockeyed, if somehow endearing, grin.

Jenny watched silently until the screen turned white. The trailer ran through the projector gate and began to flap repeatedly against the takeup reel. She was blinking away tears by the time she shut off the machine. The light faded, along with something less immediately visible. Putting the heels of both hands against her eyes, she pushed firmly and rubbed in opposite directions. Then she clasped her arms across her chest and drew in a deep, shuddery breath.

As she stumbled toward the bedroom she fought to convince herself that she hadn't done anything as immature as having gotten drunk. Her depression was due not to excessive consumption of alcohol but to the loss of something deeply felt. As yet she wasn't sure whether watching the movie again had been a good idea or not. The wine muddled both her thoughts and her emotions, which was just as well for her peace of mind.

She closed the bedroom door behind her more out of habit than necessity, crossed to the bed. A bottle of sleeping tablets waited on the nightstand. She dumped a couple into her left hand and found herself hesitating, staring at the bottle. The thought passed quickly. She put the bottle back on the table, screwing the cap back in place with careful deliberation.

The pills went down without a chaser. The wine was too tempting. Besides, she wasn't thirsty anymore. She staggered a little as she wrestled her jeans off and flopped down onto the bed. She started to remove her sweater, wondered why she was bothering, and fell back on the sheets. Consciousness fled with blissful speed.

Far out on the lake a loon cried out uncertainly. There were uncomfortable rustlings in the reeds and bushes when a sudden, unnatural breeze sprang up around them. Owls raced for the safety of their trees while nocturnal gatherers sprinted for their burrows. Something fast and white-hot was streaking across the sky, heading for the forest.

It came in low over the treetops, tumbling unsteadily. It went through the first trees as though they were made of papier-mâché, igniting the tops of those it merely brushed while incinerating the ones it struck head-on.

The fire was spreading rapidly by the time the explorer was able to emerge from his damaged craft. He scanned the burning woods, the ridge of earth that defined the rim of the impact crater his vessel had gouged. Only flames moved around him, and these he could ignore.

Finally he moved, abandoning the craft and rising to ground level. The humus-heavy soil was smoking all around him. The fire continued to spread, engulfing trees and brush in every direction.

A rising whine became audible above the excited crackling of the flames. The whine became a roar as several fighter-bombers shot past directly over the impact crater. They disappeared into the western sky. The explorer didn't doubt they'd be back. He considered his options and surroundings, and then he began to move.

Traveling with incredible swiftness, he went right through the flames. The only witness to this impossible feat was a startled, panicky deer searching for its own escape route.

The four aircraft returned and made another pass over the devastated section of forest. They were moving much too fast to pick out fine details, and in any case the fine detail they would have found most interesting had by now moved a good distance away from the conflagration.

Smaller trees the explorer cleared, large low-hanging branches he ducked beneath. He traveled with an instinctive feel for the mass and position of objects in his path. Eventually the woods gave way to a long, treeless strip of something hard and flat. It cut through the forest to left and right. Lights appeared at the far end of the road, moving toward him.

Curious, he rose and hovered, taking the time to examine the peculiar land-bound vehicle which was approaching from the north.

The young forest ranger was trying to steer the pickup and see through the forest at the same time. He held onto the wheel with one hand and the CB mike with his other. He was trying to control his emotions, but some of what he was feeling crept unbidden into what was supposed to be a professional, dispassionate report. For that he couldn't be blamed, since he'd never seen anything like what he was trying to describe before. What he didn't know was that neither had anyone else.

'I don't know what it is,' he was yelling into the mike. 'All I saw coming down was a big ball of fire. Burning airliner, maybe. Better get some choppers and maybe a tanker up here – she's building fast. Heavy smoke. Not too much wind, but you know how dry it's been up here and the undergrowth's like tinder. Just saw a firebrand leap one trail.'

The explorer watched thoughtfully from his vantage point until the pickup truck had disappeared down the road. Then he considered his position with respect to the rapidly expanding forest fire, the as yet untorched sections of woods, and the nearby lake. He began to move again. Anyone else flying low over the lake that night might have seen a strange golden glow dancing across the water. Or

19

maybe it was just the moon.

The lake was not large and the explorer soon reached the far side. There he found a single building, a small shelter of some kind with a sharply angled roof. He drifted above it, studying both the structure and the surrounding trees. There were small furry things in the growths and on the ground. They did not react to the explorer's presence. Methodically he assigned each a place within his mental catalog, estimating the intelligence and impact on the environment of every living thing he saw.

This done, he drifted low toward the artificial habitation and cautiously circled it. There was no sign of movement from within. Out in front was a sign with an example of primitive writing on it. It read FOR SALE.

Moving around the side, the explorer came upon a smaller, separate structure. It was not as well built as the other. Another of the simple land-bound vehicles rested within: a 1977 Mustang with oversized rear wheels and racing tires, chrome pipes, and a metal-flake paint job. Someone had lavished a great deal of love and care on that car, but it made no special impression on the explorer, who merely identified it as a machine similar in type and purpose to the forest ranger's pickup.

A sudden noise made him freeze. The sound was sharp and metallic, though not unpleasant. He moved toward it, relaxed when he saw that it was activated only by meteorological conditions and not intelligent purpose. The wind chimes tinkled again, loud against the night. A simple device but not without charm.

The chimes disturbed Jenny Hayden without waking her. She moaned softly in her sleep and turned over on the bed. One arm reached across the sheets as if groping for someone who wasn't there. Then the wine and pills took hold again and she fell silent once more.

The entrance to the structure was sealed, though not tightly. After locating a sufficient opening, the explorer entered by seeping through the crack under the front door, following a route often used by bugs and mosquitoes but utilizing a radically different method of locomotion.

Once inside he gathered himself again and rose to the ceiling to survey the building's interior. He recorded and analyzed.

Had he been familiar with local culture he immediately would have recognized a household in the process of being moved. Boxes half full of books and clothing and kitchenware were scattered around the room. Others were stacked neatly in one corner, sealed with packing tape, their contents marked in black crayon.

Not everything had been packed yet, however. The explorer dropped to the floor and began to inspect the unpacked goods. There was the nearly empty wine bottle, the projector, a blender, a small microwave oven, and more. The explorer paid equal attention to each item, occasionally moving one or another in order to gain a better look at back or insides. His inspection was not haphazard, however. He was looking for something in particular, looking rather anxiously in fact, and not finding it.

Unseen in the bedroom, Jenny Hayden stirred uneasily in her sleep.

The explorer drifted over to a box that rested by itself on a nearby countertop. It was a special box, though he had no way of knowing that yet. It contained a significant and eclectic potpourri of items, from fishing gear to a tennis racket and well-used balls, old sneakers which had long since outlived their usefulness, several well-frayed sweatshirts, and a handsomely blued forty-five automatic. To the explorer each was as interesting, each as significant as the other. To him the major difference between the tennis racket and the handgun was in their composition.

The counter was covered with other unpacked items. Carefully he went over a typewriter, a small color television set, more clothing, and another pile of books. One of the books lay open. It was an odd sort of book that contained no words: only pictures which had been pasted onto the otherwise blank pages.

The explorer paused there and began to examine each page of this strange book. A slight wind seemed to turn the pages in steady sequence. Most of the pictures in the front of the book were of a young boy, beginning with him as an infant and following his growth. Next to one picture was a small glassine envelope full of blond hair.

With each new page the boy grew older, becoming first a teenager and then a young man. The last portrait showed a handsome male in his mid-twenties. It was the same man Jenny had watched cavort on her movie screen earlier that evening.

The explorer had no way of knowing that, of course, but he did recognize the natural progression from the first picture to the last. As he studied the photo album something very peculiar began to happen to that last picture. A duplicate of it rose from the page and expanded into three dimensions. It rotated obediently as the explorer analyzed it in front of him before settling back onto the page resuming its original appearance.

The pages began to turn again, this time flowing backward toward the beginning as if flipped by an invisible hand. They stopped at the page holding the glassine envelope. This peeled off the paper and popped open. The lock of hair within did not fall to the floor. Instead, it began to separate, returning one by one to the envelope until only a single hair remained. The explorer concentrated on this one; estimating, appraising, deciding. He looked deeply into its substance.

Jenny wasn't able to identify what had awakened her. She blinked sleepily and lifted her head from the pillow. Another bird trying to get into the attic, she thought, or those chipmunks again. Her head hit the pillow when a distinct sound came from the living room. It was too substantial to have been made by a scurrying rodent.

She looked toward the bedroom door. There it was again, almost a crackling noise. Her gaze fell to the crack beneath the door. Faint flashes of light were filling the living room, as if someone was taking a whole series of flash pictures.

It occurred to her that she might not be alone in the cabin.

Sleepy . . . she was so sleepy. Come on, get it together, she admonished herself angrily. Too much wine, and those damn sleeping pills. She was all alone out here on the bay. All alone.

Kids. Maybe that was it. Just a couple of kids looking for videogame money. But she couldn't take the chance.

She swung her legs off the bed and sat up, fighting to clear her brain. The flashes of light continued to illuminate the floor in front of the door. Why would a thief bother taking pictures? Wavering slightly, she stood up and tiptoed around the bed to the night table on the other side. She made two grabs before getting a grip on the knob and pulling the top drawer open.

Empty. Sure it was empty. She'd been packing.

She closed the drawer and turned fearfully back to the door. The sounds in the living room continued. It didn't sound like a burglar at work, going through her things and tossing what he didn't want onto the floor. It was too regular, too even. Maybe it was a hiker who'd hurt himself and had come stumbling into her cabin in search of help. He might be lying on the floor, trying to crawl toward the sink. Sure, that was it.

But what about all the light?

A new noise reached her; a thin, uncertain whimper like a child might make. That decided her. She walked to the door and pulled it open, still trying to clear her mind from the effect of the wine and sleeping pills.

There was a figure lying on the floor. It was small and apparently uninjured. She'd been right after all. It was a child, but one much too young to be out in the woods by itself. An infant abandoned on her doorstep, just like in the movies. She took a step toward it.

And found herself starting to shake.

It was growing. The child was growing even as she looked at it. It twisted and contorted, whining with the effort it was making. Legs and arms lengthened before her

23

eyes. The torso expanded. Facial features began to crinkle and develop definition. And with each new spurt of growth it threw off a brilliant flash of light.

No sense. It made no sense at all. It was impossible. She stood there, halfway through the doorway, trying to make some sense out of what she was witnessing. She held the back of her right hand against her open mouth and seemed suddenly unable to close her jaws, just as she was unable to tear her gaze away from the thing on the floor of her living room.

It was bigger now, much bigger. In the poor light she couldn't make out many details, and each flash of light left her half blinded. The infant was long gone now. In its place a grown man lay twisting and turning on the hardwood floor.

The energy that drove the transformation began to fade, the flashes of light to become less overpowering and more infrequent. Finally they ceased altogether. The new man lay on his back on the floor, panting hard. With a visible effort he got his breathing under control and rolled clumsily onto his hands and knees. One hand opened and seven small silver gray spheres spilled out onto the floor, like a handful of silver marbles. Jenny thought she saw colors buried deep inside the silver, but given the bad light and her rapidly disintegrating sense of right and wrong she couldn't be certain of much of anything.

The man rose to his feet, facing the door, and stumbled toward it. He walked with a comical ungainliness, as if unsure how to employ his arms and legs. There were no more flashes of light. For a minute or so a faint boreal glow seemed to cling to his head. Then it too was gone.

Tripping, Jenny thought wildly. I'm tripping. What did I take with the wine besides the sleeping pills? She couldn't remember having downed anything else, but she must have. It was the only possible explanation for what was happening to her now. Unless she'd gone completely over the edge. She'd been warned of the possibility these past couple of weeks, by well-meaning friends, and she'd laughed them off. She wasn't laughing now, but she didn't feel insane, either.

Stop trying to deal with the impossible, she ordered herself. Deal with what's real, with what you *can* handle. Fact: there was a strange man stumbling around in her living room and he was stark naked and she was nearly so and she had to do something about it. She remembered fumbling through the night-table drawer and not finding what she'd been searching for. Not finding it because she'd moved the contents of the drawer into the living room so she could pack them. Her eyes searched the room. It would be over there on the breakfast counter, yes, with the rest of the sporting equipment.

Keeping her attention on the figure of the naked man, she ran for the counter and grabbed madly at the contents. Shoes, shirts, no gun. Where the hell was the gun? Please God, let me find the gun. She must have set it aside someplace. She scrabbled along the formica, brushing aside socks and shoelaces and monopoly cards, and finally picked it up. The heavy, cold metal felt familiar and reassuring in her hands and she was glad she'd taken the time to learn how to use it.

Moving back against the wall, she slapped at the light switch. The single overhead bulb came on. As the intruder turned to confront her she kept the muzzle of the forty-five pointed at his belly. His reaction to the sight of her holding the gun on him was not what she expected. There was no sudden drop into a defensive crouch, no shout of protest, no wild waving of hands. He didn't even yell 'Don't Shoot!' He just stood there by the front door and stared back at her.

And he had Scott's face.

Two

That wasn't all that she recognized. Every inch of him screamed *S cott*. He was a perfect duplicate of the man in the photo album – no, he *was* the man in the photo album, down to the smallest mole and almost healed childhood scars. Same color eyes, same hue of hair, same damaged right fingernail that he'd smashed in a construction accident.

The only thing different was the look in his eyes. They seemed to go on and on into his head, transparent lenses of infinite depth and perception. She stared into them and found herself growing dizzy.

It was all too much to try and handle. Jenny was a strong, self-possessed woman (God knows how she'd had to be strong these past many weeks), but the man standing there before her, coupled with what she imagined she'd seen happening on the floor of her cabin moments earlier, completely overwhelmed her. She staggered sideways and crumpled to the floor. The gun fell from limp fingers. She was no longer afraid because she had passed beyond fear. There was no strength left in her.

The man stared at her a moment longer before walking over to pick up the gun. She forced herself to move, willed her muscles to function as she scrambled along the wall and away from the thing that looked like Scott. When she turned once to look back over her shoulder she found that he was pointing the forty-five at her. Her mouth worked but no words came forth. She still could not understand, could not relate to the figure that stood near her, but the gun was something else again. The gun she could relate to. There was nothing alien about the forty-five. It was the most real thing in the room – solid, threatening. She huddled in a ball against the knotty pine paneling and waited for whatever might come. Was he/it going to kill her now? She was terrified to find that she didn't care. At that particularly down and dark moment in her life she would have welcomed the bullet.

Instead of pulling the trigger, the man turned and calmly resumed his examination of the living room. Finally he bent over and started to retrieve his steel marbles, or whatever they were. As he did so the muzzle of the gun dropped. At that point Jenny decided she wanted to live. She started crawling toward the front door.

Action – Reaction: he pointed the gun at her again. She froze and then retreated to her former place against the wall.

'Please don't kill me,' she found herself mumbling. Her thoughts were beginning to clear as the incredible scene she'd witnessed earlier started to recede in her memory.

He didn't reply, though she was sure he heard her. He lifted the gun and studied it closely, turning it over in his hands several times, running his fingers along the barrel, over the muzzle, the clip, and the trigger mechanism. When he concluded, he moved toward her again.

Something. She had to do something, to say something, anything, if only to hear her own voice. The silence was worse than screaming, worse than anything her words might provoke. Not that anything could be more terrifying than what she'd already seen.

'You're . . . you're not . . . Scott?'

The man halted, staring at her. At first she thought he wasn't going to answer. Then his lips kind of curled in on themselves, rippling like the gills of a fish. The mouth opened and an uncertain, feeble croak emerged.

'Skawwwt.' The expression on the familiar face didn't change, but she received a feeling of self-disgust. He tried a second time. 'Skaaht.' Again he moved toward her.

Jenny tried to make herself as small as possible, tried to

27

shrink into a little ball of flesh, wishing she could turn herself into a spider so she could flee through one of the cracks in the pine. 'No!' she shouted. It wasn't a denial; it was a moan of terror.

The man stopped again, though whether because of her shout or for reasons of his own she couldn't tell. He was very close to her now. The mouth moved again.

'*Shieh kuang. Ts'ai na . . .*'

He continued pouring out easy, fluent singsong sentences that were at once almost familiar to her and yet completely incomprehensible. It sounded like Chinese, but she was no linguist and couldn't be sure.

When she didn't respond he swallowed and tried again. '*Izvanit'yeh. Gd'yeh . . .*'

And so on again for the same length of time in yet another strange tongue. Russian? Maybe, but how could she tell, and what difference did it make anyway? He kept talking, burying her beneath a barrage of strange phrases and exotic accents, stopping and starting anew each time he saw that he wasn't getting through to her.

'*Niwie radhi – perdao – przpraszam – scuzat-mi – min faddkik – var venlig . . .*'

'Our Father who art in heaven,' Jenny began to mutter, trying to shut out the incomprehensible din, 'hallowed be thy name. Thy kingdom come, thy will be done, on Earth . . .'

She hardly dared to open her eyes because he was leaning over her now, that familiar and yet utterly alien visage only inches from her own face. She cried out and fell away from him.

Startled, he jumped backward, cleared his throat, and kept going. 'Excuse me,' he said with perfect clarity. 'As the secretary-general of the United Nations, an organization of one hundred and forty-seven member states, it is my . . .'

He droned on, but not in Scott's voice. It sounded like the voice of an older man, slightly accented. When he finished, he reached for her.

Wondering why she hadn't done so earlier, she fainted.

The explorer examined the limp female form with interest, noting the continued strength of the body's vital signs while storing this phenomenon of self-induced unconsciousness for future reference. Some kind of defensive reaction, he surmised. Definitely not an expression of either greeting or hostility. Convinced the condition wasn't being faked, he turned away from her and walked back across the floor toward the breakfast bar. He set the seven small silver spheres on the smooth surface and placed the gun next to them.

As he did so, he caught sight of himself in a full-length mirror. After another backward glance to assure himself of the native female's continued immobility, he walked up to the mirror and began to examine the form he had chosen to reconstruct and inhabit in detail.

Plain, straightforward, functional, mammalian, and primitive. Externally it was quite simple. Internal evaluation revealed that it was full of hidden and unsuspected complexities, including many of which the bipeds themselves were apparently as yet unaware. For a solid form, the explorer concluded that it showed a good deal of potential. The neurological system in particular was rich with promise.

Locomotion was achieved by means of electrical stimulation of masses of thick fibres arranged around a barely adequate skeletal superstructure. He experimented with the process, hopping from one foot to another, working the muscles of face and arms. The movements were clumsy at first but the explorer was a fast learner and the system was not difficult to master. His proficiency increased with practice and, if after five minutes of hard work he still wasn't ready to enter any break-dancing competitions, he was at least confident of his ability to manipulate the body without damaging it.

Its means of storing energy was equally as primitive as the basic design, however, and he soon found himself having to call a halt to any further physical activity until he could replenish his limited store of oxygen. Breathing hard, he rested an arm on the blender on the breakfast bar and watched with interest as the mechanical device whirred to life. When he removed his arm the blender ground to a halt. More activation of movement via electrical impulse, although in the case of the blender the motive force was supplied by fibres of copper instead of protein.

Another boxy machine rested nearby. He traced the likely source of power and plugged in the cord. The microwave oven began to hum. Instantly he analyzed the radiation it produced, found it to be simple and of low-intensity, and wondered what function the device served. When he pulled the plug the radiation ceased and the light inside the oven winked out.

His eye was caught by a device radically different in design from any he'd yet encountered. The super-eight projector was much more intriguing in appearance than the blender or oven. He crossed to the little table it rested on. A touch, and film began to move through the projection gate. Bright light threw an image on a screen across the room.

He moved his hand and the light went out, taking the moving images with it. It took a moment longer for him to locate the on-off switch and divine its function. With a flip of the switch, the movies resumed.

He was mildly startled to see moving images of the body he presently inhabited cavorting across the white plastic. *Skaht* – no, Scott, the female had called him. He studied the images intently, observing how the man moved, how he utilized the small muscles of his face to form expressions the meaning of which he had yet to learn.

Scott was doing something to the roof of a building, the same building the explorer now stood within. It was bright daylight. Something made him turn and look up from his work. He waved with one hand. He was wearing chinos, loafers, and a red-checked shirt. A baseball cap clung precariously to the back of his head.

The explorer glanced toward one of the half-filled cartons sitting on the breakfast bar, saw that it contained the same clothes the Scott on the screen had been wearing when the film was being shot. Only the baseball cap was missing.

The screen briefly went dark, then sprang to life with new footage taken of the cabin from a point farther away. A vehicle pulled into view. The explorer recognized the land machine resting in the storage building outside. Jenny sat in the driver's seat of the Mustang as it spun tight circles in the dirt in front of the cabin, kicking up dust and dry grass. She was smiling and laughing when she finally brought the car to a halt only feet from the camera.

Another shift of subject matter and Jenny was gone. The explorer looked at where she lay slumped on the floor before returning his attention to the screen. Scott was grinning into the camera. He still wore the baseball cap. In one hand he held the forty-five.

As the explorer watched silently, Scott turned to take careful aim at a row of beer cans aligned atop a wooden railing. Each time he fired the gun produced an impressive roar. The impact of something small and unseen striking the cans and knocking them off the rail was unmistakable.

The explorer watched this demonstration of casual marksmanship with particular interest. Then he walked back to the bar, picked up the automatic and aimed it at a window, pulling the trigger as he'd seen Scott do. The resultant noise was louder than expected, as was the weapon's recoil. A small, starred hole appeared in the cabin window. He turned quickly to Jenny, but the sound hadn't awakened her. Thus reassured, he turned his attention back to the still unspooling home movies.

The target practice sequence had given way to wavering shots of the cabin and the lake. Many of them included Jenny in the picture. In one series of shots she was seen trying to handfeed some animals, who were eyeing her warily. Eventually a couple of squirrels took the peanuts she was handing out. Her reaction was to squeal with childlike delight.

Something superfast and loud thundered by overhead, shaking the cabin windows and drowning out the sounds from the tiny projector speaker. This was followed by the sound of something traveling lower and slower. Helicopters,

31

though the explorer didn't know that. He listened until the mechanical noise drifted away to the east. The film ran out. He turned the projector off and regarded the woman lying on the floor for a long moment.

Then he turned and walked over to the window with the new hole in it. Across the lake and beyond a few low intervening hills the forest fire continued to rage. Now four more helicopters came into view, travelling just above treetop level. As they flew toward the flames the explorer was able to study this new type of flying device at his leisure.

When he'd seen all he wanted to he returned to the breakfast counter and picked up one of the gray spheres, then walked through the front door out onto the porch.

He stared across the quiet water of the bay toward the conflagration, put the gun down carefully on the porch railing. In his right hand the gray sphere started to glow, humming softly. The glow intensified rapidly, becoming as bright as the light of a small sun.

Air retreated from it, the wind blowing the explorer's hair straight up. The skin on his face stretched taut, new muscles tightening instinctively with the effort he was putting out as he concentrated on the sphere. Alive with a strange, cold fire and perfectly attuned to its owner, it rose from his fingers to hover in the air six inches above his open palm.

Sphere and owner communicated. Information was exchanged. Soon conversation was all one-way as the explorer imprinted his thoughts and observations on the malleable interior of the gray marble.

'Emergency transmission. First Lander to Base Ship. Standard communications inoperable. Observation craft destroyed. Environment benign save for instinctively hostile reactions of dominant local species. Form of reaction equally primitive but effective.

'Do not undertake retrieval in this area. Avoidance of intensification of hostilities is paramount concern as per all relevant directives. I have completed temporary endomorphic assimilation with genetic duplicate of local dominant life form. Code is not complex but variations are interesting,

32

untapped potential of system more so. Will study while proceeding to retrieval point. Proceed standard as per . . .'

Jenny moaned to herself, lifted her head and opened her eyes. Something, there was something important, but she'd forgotten it. Something had happened. She'd started watching those damned old home movies against her better judgment, and she'd had too much wine to drink, and something else. Something crazy insane impossible . . .

She remembered, wildly searched the room. There was no sign of her imagined intruder. A dream, sure, wine and sleeping pills and emotional upset and that's all it had been, a cock-eyed dream.

Which didn't explain the intense glow that was lighting up the front porch.

She got on her knees and crawled toward the nearest window. Halfway across the floor she remembered that she didn't have anything on below the waist except a pair of panties and that her knees weren't exactly callused. Carefully she climbed to her feet and walked the rest of the way.

Maybe this was all part of the nightmare. Maybe she'd just left the porch light on when she'd come inside to reminisce, just reminisce and get good and drunk.

She pressed her face against the glass, looked to her left, and sucked in her breath. The Scott who wasn't Scott was standing next to the railing. His hair was flowing skyward, as though he was standing on a powerful fan. Floating just above his outstretched right palm was a tiny burning globe. A strange musical sound came from the naked figure and the globe seemed to respond to it. All her fears returned tenfold. But she couldn't stop staring.

'Rendezvous third dawn-break, original retrieval area. Emergency transmission concluded.'

The musical emanation stopped. The glowing sphere began to rise, slowly at first. When it reached a point some hundred feet or so above the calm water of the bay, it suddenly accelerated. Save for the miniature sonic boom it produced as it shot heavenward, she would have thought it had simply disappeared.

33

The sound broke her paralysis and she was able to start backing toward the bedroom, feeling her way as she retreated through the bedroom doorway, her eyes never leaving the front entrance until she was safely inside. She closed the door behind her, locked it, and began searching through her clothing. When she didn't find what she was looking for there she moved on to her purse, then her jacket. She finally found the car keys in a side pocket, right where she'd left them. She held them as tightly as she would have the forty-five.

Without pausing to slip on her pants, which she tossed over an arm, she opened the bedroom window and climbed over the sill. It was only a short drop to the ground.

There was gas in the tank. She'd filled up before turning off the highway, not wanting to find herself stuck at the cabin without a quick way out. Her intention had been to be ready to flee from unbearable memories. Now she found herself running from something much worse.

Surely she could get the car started and backed out of the carport before he could react! It was an older car but it was as finely tuned as a Tina Turner song. Scott had always kept it tuned perfectly. Scott had always . . .

She turned the corner toward the carport and felt strong hands on her shoulders.

No more fainting, not now, not again. That wouldn't make the nightmare go away. So she started screaming instead. If he'd slapped her, or yelled at her to stop it, or thrown her to the ground, she would have quit. But he did none of those things. He just stood there holding onto her and staring at her out of those strangely deep eyes.

Her hysteria was washed out by the rumble of a forestry service helicopter as it thumped past overhead. It was on its way to join its brethren in fighting the fire across the lake. Now the man who looked like Scott but wasn't a man shook her. Not hard, but sufficient to choke off her screams.

She gagged, caught her breath enough to choke out, 'Who are you? *What* are you? What do you want with me? Please, let me alone.'

34

'We go,' he said. It was Scott's voice this time, just slightly different. Just as the man holding her was slightly different.

Another helicopter trundled past. She waved frantically at it but the pilot wasn't looking downward. His attention was on the fiery destination ahead. He was talking to his copilot, estimating how many minutes remained before they reached the flames and trying to decide from a combination of visual observations and radio reports where best to dump the load of fire retardant chemicals they carried in the chopper's belly.

The man who looked like Scott turned and pointed toward the carport. 'We go,' he said again. He headed back into the house, pulling her along with him. Inside she watched as he dressed himself in the chinos, checkered shirt, and a windbreaker. After a moment's thought he added socks and loafers. Underwear he ignored.

Then he escorted her back to the car, watched carefully as she slid behind the wheel, and climbed in next to her. He gave her no chance to lock him out. Not that she would have considered doing so anyway. Not while he still had the gun.

He watched closely as she turned the key in the ignition. Her hand was shaking and she made a bad job of what ordinarily was a simple task. The battery ran down despite her best efforts to get the engine to turn over. Maybe Scott had kept the engine tuned up, but the battery was old and probably in need of replacement.

'It's been sitting here for days,' she told him. 'And the motor's old. And the battery needs replacing, and I . . .'

She broke off. He was staring at her uncomprehendingly. 'What's wrong?'

'What's wrong?' She muttered to herself. 'I'll tell you what's wrong. Two downers and a jug of wine.' She slapped herself. It worked in cartoons. Maybe it would work now.

'Jenny, dammit, wake up.'

No luck. He was still there, staring at her. As she waited he raised an arm and gestured toward the dirt road that led away from the lake. There was a halting insistence in his voice.

'We must go. Now.'

She tried the key again. The engine growled. She was frightened and tired and dazed and she wasn't thinking her actions through. The end result was that she flooded the engine. When it died this time it sounded final. The thin sharp smell of gasoline filled the car.

His hand dropped to the automatic resting in his lap. She was near collapse from panic.

'I'm sorry, I'm sorry! I can't get it started. I tried, but I can't. Can't you smell it? It's flooded. We'll have to wait.' Her eyes were darting rapidly from his face to the hand now cradling the forty-five.

Suddenly he leaned over and touched the ignition key. Or maybe he didn't touch it. Maybe he only touched the ignition plate. She was never certain, then or afterward.

The engine rumbled, turned over once, twice. It caught on the third try, the big 387 under the hood coming to loud life. It idled smoothly as she threw her companion an uncertain look, then turned resolutely away from him. If she didn't pay attention to her driving she'd like as not end up killing them both.

Still feeling his eyes on her she backed out, shifted gears and sent them bouncing down the narrow access road that led away from the bay.

They worked their way through mud and over potholes until they finally came to the intersection where the access lane met blacktop. Jenny slowed to a halt. She was glad of the solid, unyielding plastic of the steering wheel beneath her fingers. It gave her something to hold onto, and she badly needed something to hold onto. Reality was a half-memory. She was trapped in a persistent nightmare that was solidifying around her like stale Jell-o. It was hard to breathe, harder still to remain calm. If anything even slightly out of the ordinary had happened to that steering wheel, if it had turned suddenly soft and rubbery in her hands or sported a couple of leering eyes or gone floating off skyward like a small gray sphere she'd recently seen do just that, she was absolutely certain she would have gone quite insane.

It did none of those things. It stayed a steering wheel, the familiar smooth plastic curve cool inside the curl of her fingers. The engine purred softly beneath the hood, the leather seat was warm against her back. Everything was as it should be. Everything, except the character sitting next to her cradling the deadly automatic in his lap.

'Why do you stop?'

Compared to what her keeper had said so far, the question amounted to a veritable speech.

She gestured at the intersection. 'Which way do you want to go? Left or right? East or west? Does it matter? Should I just drive?' Silently she prayed that he'd leave the decision up to her. It would amount to a confession of ignorance of his surroundings – though she already suspected he wasn't a local. If he just wanted to drive aimlessly she would turn left and head for the nearest big town.

He appeared to be debating with himself. Finally, and with obvious reluctance, he reached into one of the windbreaker's pockets and withdrew another of the mysterious gray spheres. She wondered if it, too, was going to vanish into the night sky.

'What's that?' she asked, unable to restrain her curiosity. As usual, he ignored her question. Not that she expected an answer, but the sound of her own voice was better than complete silence.

He was staring at it intently. It began to hum, a purely mechanical noise, but not an unpleasant one. Like the one she'd seen him holding on the porch, it also started to glow, though not nearly as intensely. It did not rise out of his hands.

Instead, it exploded.

She threw up both hands in front of her face, trying to shield her eyes. There was no need. The explosion produced neither sound, heat, radiation, or damaging light. When she lowered her hands she found herself gaping at an image splashed across the inside of the windshield. It was so realistic she momentarily had to grab the wheel to steady herself. Then she realized they hadn't been suddenly transported to a point in space hundreds of miles up.

The windshield had been replaced by a holographic projection of startling depth and realism. She recognized the image instantly. It was the continent of North America, rendered in every perfect detail. It was not a map, but rather a reproduction of some kind of miraculous photograph.

As she stared the image shrank until it encompassed only the continental United States, swerved and compressed still further until it showed the Southwest. She gulped and hung onto the wheel anyway. Watching the shifting image was like falling.

Specific geographic features were brought into sharp relief with the aid of superimposed bright colors. There was an isolated, exceptionally high mountain, a series of descending plateaus, and in the center of the projection an odd circular canyon – no, a crater. She was sure it was some kind of crater.

The image enlarged slightly but remained focused on the brightly outlined crater. She wished she'd studied her geography better in school.

Her keeper reached up, into the projection itself. The outline of the crater pulsed when his finger touched it. 'Here.'

She gaped at him. 'You wanna be driven to that place? Is that it?' And she'd been hoping he'd ask to be dropped off somewhere nearby.

'Yes. That place.' He looked relieved at having made his point. 'Wanna be driven that place. You know where that place is?'

She forced herself to consider the projection. 'Well, if that's Baja California down there, and up there's Salt Lake, then over here,' she reached up to touch the image and was inordinately pleased with herself for not twitching when her finger passed into and through the seemingly solid surface, 'this has to be the Grand Canyon. The place you want to go is further east, but it's still got to be in – it's hard to tell without state lines on your map. I'm not real good at this.'

'State lines?'

'Never mind. What you're pointing to is, like, Arizona maybe.'

He nodded vigorously. 'Yes, wanna be driven there. Arizona-maybe.'

'Why Arizona?'

'Driven there. Now.'

She sighed tiredly. Some of the fear was beginning to give way to curiosity. You couldn't stay terrified forever, after all. For one thing, it was too exhausting. And it seemed like as long as she did as he asked, he wasn't going to hurt her. If his original motive had been robbery he already would have taken what he wanted, including the car, and left. If rape, there was no need to drive all the way to Arizona to perpetrate the act. That left only kidnapping, but that didn't make much sense either. And why haul her all the way to Arizona, when she might have a dozen chances to escape during the long drive?

And there was his manner. She didn't know what else to call it. What at first she'd taken for brusqueness now seemed more like plain ignorance. Ignorance of the language, of local customs, of the simplest things. She decided he had to be a foreigner of some kind – but weird. And what about the glowing spheres, and this incredible photomap, and the hair blowing straight up into the air?

What about his face? Scott's face.

She followed his instructions and took a right out onto the blacktop, still worried but no longer petrified with fear. She'd always considered herself a sensible woman, and none of the events of the past hour made the slightest bit of sense.

'If this isn't a dream,' she muttered aloud, 'then I'm in big trouble.' He might have been expected to comment on that, to say something to the effect that she was right and it wasn't a dream. But as with everything else she said he ignored it. He just sat there, holding onto the gun, staring out at the road and drinking in the scenery. Often he would turn sharply, as though he saw something in the black wall of the forest, and she had the feeling he could see just as well in the dark as he could during the day.

* * *

The army helicopter was an S-76: big, clumsy, slow, reliable. It went thrashing along above the forest, disturbing the peaceful Wisconsin dawn and sending a flock of startled geese splashing in panic across the mirrorlike surface of the lake.

Its pilot studied his electronic coordinator, which relieved him of personal responsibility for finding out where the hell he was, and compared the readings with what he could see of the terrain ahead. He turned to his copilot.

'Ten minutes.'

'What say?' The copilot was bouncing and jerking about in his seat like someone possessed by an incurable muscular disease. The pilot, who did not approve of the cause of this seated version of Saint Vitus's dance, would have been more likely to compare it to a mental deficiency.

He cured it by reaching across and yanking the stereo earphones off the copilot's head. 'I said, ten minutes!' He nodded toward the back of the chopper. 'Better wake the cargo.'

'Right.' The copilot set his tape player aside, along with more official sound equipment, and headed toward the back of the helicopter.

In the communications compartment the radioman was seated at his position, listening to KWFJ out of Milwaukee and wishing he had enough range to pick up Detroit. But it was better than that station they'd hit on earlier, the one that played polka music twenty-four hours 'round the clock. The radioman would rather listen to the music of the Gulag, and unlike Gamble, he didn't pull enough rank to rate bringing his personal music box on board.

'What's up?' he asked the copilot.

'We're getting close. Time for all good passengers to start earning their keep, I guess. Or whatever it is this dude's supposed to do out here.' He nodded toward the rumpled figure sprawled out on the nearby cot. 'Wonder who he is to rate this kind of service?'

The radioman shrugged. 'Beats me, man.' He returned to his monitoring.

The copilot moved past him, put a hand on the sleeper's shoulder and shook firmly. He didn't know much about their passenger and sole cargo, but he was willing to give anyone who could climb aboard an S-76 and instantly fall asleep the benefit of the doubt.

'About that time, Mister Shermin.' When no response was forthcoming he gave the shoulder another nudge.

Mark Shermin blinked, rubbed at his eyes as he sat up. 'Oh. Okay.' He tried to see past the radioman and out the side window. 'We there already?'

'Already? We've been in the air for almost an hour, Mister Shermin.' The radioman felt a twinge of sympathy for the civilian. Poor guy. No telling when was the last chance he had to sleep in his own bed. 'My name's Lemon.' He reached down and picked up a thermos, scrounged until he'd located an almost clean cup. 'Coffee?'

'Thanks,' said Gamble, reaching for it.

'Not you, disco-brain. Get back forward where you belong.' The copilot grinned at him and made his way back to the forward compartment.

'Thanks.' Shermin accepted thermos and cup and poured himself six ounces of black liquid. A couple of swallows and his brain began to function again. Colombia's legal narcotic. He found himself considering the complex of communications equipment as he sipped.

'Listen sergeant, I know you can handle all kinds of exotic transmissions and high-speed signals with that, but what about more commonplace stuff? Can you pick up the regular police bands on that thing?'

'No problem. Why? You bored already?'

'It's not that. Kind of has to do with what I'm out here for. I'm interested in anything really freaky that's been going on around here. You know; far out, weird, bizarre. It's all related to what I do.'

Lemon smiled. 'I know a lady you'd like.'

Shermin grinned back at him, finished the rest of the coffee and set the cup aside. 'Better start getting ready, I guess. What's it like, where we're going?'

The radioman was fiddling with his instrumentation. 'Like most of Wisconsin: trees, lakes, nice country. You want weird and far out? Man, you're going to get weird and far out. Just promise me one thing, okay?'

'What's that?'

'After you get through doing your studies or digging or photographing or whatever it is you're out here to do, you let me know what the hell's going on.'

'If I can.' Shermin got off the cot, took his contamination suit off the wall rack and started struggling into it. Lemon watched the procedure thoughtfully while continuing to monitor his instruments.

'Hey, what's that for? They didn't give us nothing like that when they sent us out here to recon.'

'You've been to the site already, then?' Shermin pulled the sleeves of the suit up his arm, made sure the elastic at the wrists was secure and started slipping on the gloves.

'Yeah, once.'

'Did you set down in the area?'

Lemon shook his head. 'Just circled and took pictures.'

'Then you wouldn't need something like this.' He zipped up the front of the suit and checked to make sure the gloves were secured to the sleeves at the wrists. 'What do you think?'

'Flashy. You look like the baked potato that ate Chicago. Seriously, you think you're going to need it, down there?'

'I hope not, but I wouldn't want to guess wrong and find myself without it. I might like to have kids some day, you know?'

The last vestige of the radioman's smile vanished. 'I hear you.'

By the time the S-76 rumbled into the impact area the chopper's crew was all business. Smoke still rose from blackened trees. The forest fire had burned briefly but intensely, helped along by a gusting breeze. It was out now only because the forestry service and local fire brigades had jumped on it hard and fast.

Shermin tucked his helmet under an arm. Local monitors

already on the scene would inform him if it was necessary. He peered out the side window as they hovered above the devastated area. It was immediately apparent that something more than a simple forest fire had damaged this part of southern Wisconsin.

In addition to the trees incinerated in the fire there was a long black swath that ran through otherwise untouched forest from west to east. Something had cut through the woods with irresistible force. The path of destruction ended near the center of the fire and was centered on a shallow but still impressive impact crater. Around the crater trees hadn't been burned as much as they'd been flattened, their needles and leaves and smaller branches blasted off.

'Jesus,' Shermin muttered.

'Looks like somebody set off a big one, huh?' Lemon commented without looking up from his equipment.

'Something like that,' was Shermin's noncommittal reply. He knew full well that no bomb had caused this havoc, but his employers would crucify him if he started volunteering his professional opinion to the uniformed help. So he kept his thoughts to himself. Lemon took the hint and didn't ask a second time.

Two more helicopters were in view, flying circles around the crater, as the S-76 settled down in the impact area. They were smaller Hueys, flying patrol. Farther off Shermin saw a fully armed Apache keeping watch on the lake. Woe to any curious pilots of private aircraft who unwisely strayed into this off-limits chunk of airspace.

'Watch yourself out there, man,' said Lemon as Shermin stepped out, still cradling his helmet under one arm.

'Yeah, sure.' Useless warning, nice thought. There was nothing here to watch out for. Or was there?

That was one of the things he'd been sent to find out.

Air-force insignia decorated the shoulders of several men working around the edge of the crater. They wore suits similar to Shermin's and went at their assignments with single-minded dedication and in complete silence. The Geiger counters and similar paraphernalia they were using

43

looked right up to date, Shermin decided.

He was wondering whether or not he should match their attire by donning his own helmet when an air-force major climbed out of the crater in front of him. The officer also wore a suit, but like Shermin, carried his helmet. Shermin breathed a sigh of relief. He suffered from slight claustrophobia. Not having to wear the helmet was the nicest thing that had happened to him in two days.

The officer saw him standing there and swerved to meet him. That wasn't surprising. Shermin knew he was expected.

They shook hands. 'I'm Major Bell, Cletus Bell.'

'Mark Shermin.' The major didn't ask what he was doing there. No one got within five miles of the impact crater unless they'd already been cleared at a much higher level than the major usually dealt with.

Shermin started toward the ridge of earth that ringed the excavation. 'It's clean?'

'No radioactivity, if that's what you mean. You'd get more rads standing next to a microwave. No bacteria readings, either.'

'That's no surprise.' Shermin nodded toward the crater. 'Even assuming there were any they would've been vaporized in the first flash of heat during impact.'

Bell went silent for a moment, finally asked, 'You're attached to National Security?'

'Not very.' He considered. Bell had a right to know more. He wasn't a chopper radioman. 'I just work for them occasionally. On loan, like a library book. Didn't you know that we consultants really run the country? Actually, my full time interests lie with SETI.'

Bell frowned. 'You're a whale expert?'

Shermin smiled. 'No, that's CETI. SETI is the Search for Extraterrestrial Intelligence.'

The major's eyebrows rose. 'Things must be kind of slow between Spielberg films. So they're sending you guys out on meteorites now, huh? I thought they'd send a geologist.' He nodded distastefully toward the crater. 'I can tell you now there's no diamonds.'

'Diamonds?' Now it was Shermin's turn to frown.

'These guys think it's a meteorite, everybody starts looking for diamonds. Heat and pressure, carbon, and slow wits.' He shook his head. 'So you're looking at meteorites now? I wouldn't think someone with your interests would find them worth checking out.'

'Only the ones that change course.'

That brought Bell up short. 'Change course? Can they do that?'

'This one did. Or else some airhead at NORAD misread a glitch on his instrumentation.'

Bell indicated the activity around the crater, the men busy in their decontamination suits, the circling helicopters, the others searching methodically through the woods for they knew not what but searching diligently nonetheless.

'If so I'll bet he's sweating now. I didn't think they could move troops this fast anymore. Something's got somebody excited.' He stared straight at Shermin. 'Do they have reason to be?'

Shermin shrugged. 'Beats me. I just got here.' He nodded toward the crater. 'Let's have a look.'

'Sure. Not a whole lot to see.'

They climbed the earthen berm and looked down into the hole. Lying at the bottom of the crater was a black, irregularly shaped object about the size of a dead Cadillac. A couple of silver-suited airmen stood atop it. One of them was hefting something but Shermin's view was blocked by his companion. Hoses and thick cables coiled around the feet of both men and ran up the crater wall, then down the outside and off to parts unseen.

They started down, Shermin moving carefully and studying the carbonized soil as he descended. A loud noise suddenly filled the excavation. Shermin identified it instantly. Now he knew what the first airman was holding. It was a drill, and a big one.

He gaped at the airmen, then turned angrily to Bell. 'What's going on here? What the hell are they doing?'

'I told you: diamonds. Besides, nobody's told us what not to do, and I've been getting damn tired standing around watching my men picking dead birds and squirrels out of

45

the underbrush.' He nodded toward the two men. 'They're trying to see what's in there.'

'No one authorized that.'

'Like I said, no one forbade it. Besides, we checked it out with probe poles and the damn thing sounded hollow to me. We walked all over it when we started checking it for radiation. I'm not the only one who thought it sounded hollow.'

'That's idiotic, major. There's no such thing as a hollow . . .'

His words were washed out by the noise of the drill as they began to approach the object. Suddenly one of the men stumbled forward, nearly fell. His buddy steadied him as the drill broke through the object's exterior. A thin jet of nearly colorless vapor hissed skyward. The volume diminished rapidly and there was no noticeable odor.

Shermin froze, his eyes wide. Bell broke out in a shit-eating grin but forebore from saying anything – for about ten seconds.

'You were about to say?'

'Jesus H. Christ.' Shermin looked paralyzed, finally shook himself. 'Nothing. I wasn't going to say anything.' He was staring in fascination at the object lying at the bottom of the crater. His thoughts were going eighty miles a minute. The two airmen had put the drill aside and were bending over, peering intently at the spot on the surface where they'd been working. They were muttering to one another but not loudly enough for Shermin to hear what they were saying.

A couple of raindrops pelted his face. They were followed by a deluge. The storm seemed to have materialized out of nowhere. Moments earlier the sky had been clear and bright, with only a few isolated cumulus in sight. Now it was like the monsoon season. Shermin and Bell tried to shield themselves from the torrential and unseasonable downpour with their helmets.

'What now?' Bell asked him.

Shermin nodded toward the object. 'Let's get this thing out of here.'

Three

The music helped. The men didn't seem to object to her listening, or to her changing the stations whenever the mood suited her. Each time the news came on she quickly switched to fresh music, and he didn't seem to mind that either.

What had been a lovely morning turned suddenly sour with the appearance of raindrops on the windshield. It matched her mood.

'Rain,' she said conversationally. It produced the usual response from her passenger, which was to say, nothing at all. He just stared blankly at her as if waiting to see what she might say next. He wasn't completely indifferent to her, however. He still kept one hand securely on the handle of the automatic.

'Windshield wipers.' She indicated the rain, which was beginning to streak the glass and blur the view ahead. 'I have to turn on the windshield wipers.'

'Windshield wipers,' he repeated. He said it perfectly. He only had to say something once to get it right.

She reached down and flipped them on. The road ahead reemerged from the moisture. The steady swish-swish of the blades was relaxing, like the music. Another sign of normalcy in a world that had suddenly gone topsy-turvy on her. Another sign of sanity.

They were coming to a small town, one of hundreds of identical little communities dotting central and southern Wisconsin. It was large enough to rate a signal in the center of town, at the main intersection. As they approached, the light shifted from green to yellow.

'Stoplight,' she told him.

'Stoplight.' Another echo. She decided on an experiment.

Instead of slowing down, she floored the accelerator. Her passenger didn't react, didn't yell for her to stop, didn't so much as blink. Just sat quietly and stared as she raced the light. It went to red before she reached the intersection. She held her breath as the Mustang ran the signal, but theirs was the only vehicle in sight.

The town was big enough to warrant the stoplight, but if there was a cop around he was conspicuous by his absence. She didn't slow down again until they had passed the last house and were back among the trees. Repeated glances into the rearview mirror revealed only empty road behind them. There was no sign of hoped-for flashing red lights, no sound of a closing siren.

And still he continued to ignore her. Did he know what she'd been trying to do back there and had he simply decided not to pay any attention, or was he so foreign, so ignorant of local customs that he didn't know the difference between a yellow light and a red one? She wasn't sure which to believe.

Maybe she ought to give in and listen to some news. The clock on the dash said it was almost six. If her abductor was some kind of dangerous foreign agent or escaped madman or something, maybe there'd be something on the news about him. The continued not-knowing was worse than anything the broadcaster might say. She found herself wishing he was nothing more than a Russian spy on the run, or some scientist who'd gone over the edge and maybe shot a couple of his colleagues.

That much at least she could make sense of.

The music segued into a station signature tune, then to the sound of a rooster crowing, and finally a voice. Still no reaction from her passenger.

'Up and at 'em, folks,' said the cheery voice of the DJ. 'This is station WDUL, Duluth, Minnesota, bringing you the six A.M. news. World news, commodity index and farm

48

prices following the weather. But first, what's been happening in our neck o' the woods.

'No folks, those of you who saw that flash in the sky last night, you weren't imagining things. It wasn't the end of the world, neither, and it wasn't a burning airliner. No sir.'

Jenny found her eyes edging away from the road and back over toward her silent companion. Words continued to pour from the speaker. She was looking at him differently now, and her expression began to alter as the DJ's voice rambled on.

'Nope,' he continued in his folksy, bucolic fashion, 'according to the AP wire, one of the biggest meteors to strike our little old planet Earth in the past eighty years hit last night right here in our own backyard, near Ashland and not far from Chequamegon Bay, right over the border. So for you folks who called in to say that you saw a flying saucer land over there, this ought to take care of . . .'

Jenny didn't want to hear any more. She reached out and turned the radio off. The road bent sharply to the left. Between her need to shut off the flow of reportage and simultaneously keep an eye on her passenger she nearly drove off the pavement. The car's wild gyrations didn't faze him in the least. Why should they, she thought? She stifled the laughter that was building inside her because she recognized it as the incipient hysteria it was.

Foreign? Oh, that was funny, that was! He was a foreigner all right. It didn't explain what he was doing with Scott's face and body, but it explained a helluva lot of other things. Like his silence, and that unnaturally direct stare, and his ignorance of things as commonplace as red lights and windshield wipers. It explained what she'd seen in the living room and on her front porch last night. It explained just about everything – except what they were doing together driving a souped-up '77 Mustang south toward Arizona.

She looked from the radio to him and back again, hoping he – it, whatever – at least had enough sense to make the connection. 'That was about you, wasn't it? That flash, that

49

meteor, that was you coming down. You really are some kind of Martian or something, aren't you?'

Silence and indifference.

'What do you want here?' The questions came pouring out of her. 'What are you doing? What do you want with me? Where did you learn to speak English?' A car was coming toward them. She ignored it. 'Come on, damn you. Say something! I know you can talk a little bit, anyway. Where'd you learn English?'

Now he did look at her, but when he opened his mouth it was a different voice from the one that had spoken to her before which emerged. Not that it was unfamiliar, and the words were understandable. It wasn't Russian or Chinese, and it wasn't the old man's voice.

It was Mick Jagger's, or a remarkable facsimile. 'I can't get no, satisfaction,' the man sang to her. He was as straight-faced as if he were serenading a high-school sweetheart.

'That does it,' she muttered grimly. She closed her eyes, hit the brakes with both feet, and threw the wheel hard left, sending the Mustang skidding crazily toward the approaching vehicle. Caught off guard, her passenger went tumbling into the dashboard.

The driver of the van locked up his own brakes, sending the bigger vehicle into a wild skid as he fought to miss the oncoming Mustang. The end result was that both of them ended up sliding sideways toward each other. There was a metallic *bang* as doors contacted, slid apart, and caught again on rear fenders. The van's left taillight exploded in a shower of red plastic. Metal crumpled. The Mustang skewed around in a full three-sixty before coming to a stop on the shoulder.

The van was owned by a young and presently extremely upset man named Heinmuller. As soon as he managed to get both his breath and his bus under control he locked the parking brake. Then he reached under the front seat and brought out a big lug wrench. Piling out of the van, he paused to check his custom paint job. His blood pressure rose steadily as he noted the gouges in the lacquer, the marks on one mag wheel, and the missing curb indicator. That much he could have lived with, but the twisted rear fender and busted taillight were something else again. It wasn't just the broken red plastic cover, either. The metal had been punched in and wires were showing. Between that and the fender he had a major project on his hands.

One thing for sure: he wasn't going to pay for it.

He turned and shouted angrily toward the Mustang, which still rested where it had skidded to a halt on the shoulder behind him.

'You crazy sons of bitches! What's the matter with you? Look what you did to my van. You want to play chicken on the highway, why don't you find somebody else to pick on?' He gestured at the damaged fender. 'You see this? Who's gonna pay for this?' When no response was forthcoming from his assailant, he picked up a rock lying by the side of the road and threw it at the other car. 'Come on, own up to it, and you damn well better have insurance!'

The explorer blinked, shook his head. He'd been stunned by the collision with the dash. Now he turned to see Jenny trying to scramble out the door. The gun had tumbled to the floor and lay somewhere out of sight beneath the seat. There was no time to go hunting for it. He grabbed at her, still unbalanced by the concussion he'd suffered.

Heinmuller had started toward the Mustang, holding the big lug wrench tightly in his right hand. If they wouldn't come to him, he'd sure as hell go to them. He could understand the reason for their continued silence, but if they thought he was going to shine it on they had another thing coming. He was prepared for just about anything: a fight, confrontation with somebody strung out on dope, a bunch of frightened, drunken teenagers.

The one thing he wasn't prepared for was to see the door of the Mustang burst open and an attractive young woman come staggering out. She saw him and instead of offering an apology or trying to run away, she took a step toward him and started screaming at the top of her lungs.

An attack he could have coped with. An injury from

51

within the car he could have coped with. The one thing he wasn't ready to deal with was a wild cry for help. He stopped in his tracks.

A man followed her out of the car and locked his arms around her. They started scrambling around, kind of wrestling and yet not quite fighting. Heinmuller stared at them and they both stared back.

'Help me, please!' the woman was shouting.

'I send greetings!' the guy yelled, with equal intensity. He smiled even as he continued to tussle with the woman who, Heinmuller noted absently, wasn't bad looking at all.

The near collision and the damage to his precious van temporarily shoved to the back of his thoughts by this new situation, he stood watching them while trying to decide what to do next.

'What the hell's going on here?' he finally asked them. 'What's with you two?' The last thing he wanted to do was insert himself into the middle of some serious domestic quarrel.

'I'm being kidnapped!' the woman insisted.

'Greetings!' said her companion again.

Heinmuller frowned. They were fighting, that was for sure, but not as husband and wife. But the guy neither looked nor acted like a kidnapper. Something mighty cockeyed was happening here and he wasn't sure he wanted any part of it.

But if she was telling the truth.

He raised the lug wrench and started toward them, keeping his eyes fixed on the man. He was still wary of both of them. This might be some kind of scam, a show designed to lull his suspicions so they could steal his van. But the more he watched the woman struggling the less he thought that was the case.

'Let her go, pal, or I'll give you greetings,' he finally said.

As he drew near, the man reached into a pocket of his windbreaker. Heinmuller dropped to a cautionary crouch, but the guy didn't have a gun. It was only some kind of ball bearing or something. As soon as he saw that his would-be

52

opponent wasn't armed he resumed his advance. The man held the hand holding the gray sphere out toward him.

'All right, buddy, you asked for it. I told you to let go of her.' Heinmuller decided to hit the guy on the arm. That ought to make him loosen his grasp.

The man's fingers contracted, breaking the gray sphere he held. There was an explosive crackle. It sounded like a power transformer blowing up. A bright ball of light formed around the man's fist.

'Hey – ouch!' Heinmuller flung the wrench away as though it had bit him. Suddenly it was glowing a bright, cherry red. Behind him a forty-foot pine exploded like a torch. Both tree and wrench had been in a straight line with the man's fist, but Heinmuller didn't make the connection. His gaze traveled from his hand to the roaring blaze behind him to the now white-hot lug wrench. As he stared at it the steel dissolved into tiny metal balls of evaporating metal which sizzled and vanished into the air like spit on a hot stove. Seconds later there was only steaming earth where the wrench had been lying.

Heinmuller gaped at the spot for another moment, to convince himself that he hadn't imagined it, then turned and ran like hell for his van. Jenny slumped as the badly frightened young man burned rubber as he disappeared down the highway.

Her captor helped her back onto her feet. His gentle touch even while fighting to keep her under control was just one more addition to the mass of contradictions that he was composed of. She didn't scream anymore. There was no one around to hear her now, besides which she was more awed than frightened. When she turned to stare at him it was clear he wasn't even upset by her attempt to escape. His expression was unchanged.

'What did you do? How did you do that?' She pointed toward the ground where the wrench had – the only description she could think of that fit was 'vanished.'

He said nothing, directed her gently but firmly back into the car. This time he climbed in front of her and was waiting

53

with the gun tucked back in the waistband of his chinos when she slid in behind the wheel. He gestured down the road. As far as he was concerned they might have stopped for a quick look at the scenery.

'Okay, okay,' she said tiredly. 'I know. Arizona-maybe.'

'Yes, Arizona-maybe,' he repeated. He paused a moment before adding, 'Define "okay."'

'Okay means all right, you win. We'll do it your way.'

He turned away from her and resumed his Buddhalike stare out the front window. As he did so the false smile she'd put on her face faded and she muttered under her breath, 'In a pig's eye we will.' She shifted into drive and the Mustang pulled back out onto the pavement.

The huge Sikorsky workhorse hovered over the center of the impact crater. Several thick cables hung from its belly into the hole. Workers on the ground attached the dangling lines to the steel cage that had been built around the blackened object in the crater's center.

Mark Shermin watched until he was sure both cables and cage would do their job without snapping. Then he turned and jogged back to his own waiting helicopter.

Once inside he turned back to the crater. The Sikorsky's two big engines revved up. The meteor, or whatever it was, went up easily on the skycrane's winch. He followed their progress until both chopper and cargo had disappeared over the threes. Then he turned to the waiting radioman and nodded.

Lemon punched in a numerical sequence on the keyboard in front of him, waited until a series of lights winked to life atop the readout board. He spoke into the mike.

'Communications Central, this is Project Visitor, Chequamegon Sighting. I have Mister Shermin here for you.' A pause, then he glanced back at his waiting charge. 'Your director's on the line.'

Shermin recognized George Fox's voice instantly. The director was talking to someone in the same room with him. 'Are we on scramble? Okay.' Then, more loudly, 'All right, Shermin, what is it?'

'I don't know.'

'How can you not know? You're not paid not to know, Shermin. I can not know myself. I've got a whole building full of bozos working for me back in Washington who don't know. So don't let me hear it from you.'

'What I mean, sir, is that I've an idea what it is but I'd rather not speculate until I've had a chance to examine it fully. We just lifted it out of here. It's on its way back to the base and I'm getting ready to follow it in.

'I'll tell you this much. If it *is* a meteor, it's the funniest one I've ever seen. It's not iron or nickel or any kind of stony matter, though again, I don't want to commit myself firmly until we've had proper analyses run on it. I'm not even sure the composition is metallic. For one thing it's got some kind of funny glaze all over it. Most of it burned off on reentry, but there's still enough left to analyze. Some kind of weird ceramic or something. Like I said, it's awfully early for speculation. I want to run a piece of it through the lab. Spectrograph, specific gravity, the usual stuff.

'The other thing, sir, is that it's hollow.'

'How do you know? About the hollow, I mean.'

'They drilled a little hole in it. Before I got here. Somebody got impatient. I didn't authorize it and there was nobody here to tell them otherwise, but in any case it's too late now. It's done, and it doesn't appear to have damaged anything. Not as far as I can tell just by looking at it, anyways.'

'So what you're telling me,' Fox said slowly, 'is that my first instinct was right. It's Soviet space-garbage, albeit a new variety. Maybe we've lucked into something valuable. If it was important, they'd do everything to make us think otherwise, up to and including denying that it's theirs. Maybe they're hoping they can get their people onto it and recover it or blow it up or something before we've had a chance to poke around inside it.'

'No sir, with all due respect to your opinion, I don't think that's it. I don't think it's Soviet.'

'Then what the devil have you got out there, Shermin?'

'I'll know more in a few hours, sir. Like I said, it's on the way out of here now. I'll have it cleaned up at the base and then covered up and shipped out. A lab's being set up in Madison and everything should be ready by the time I get there with the object.'

In his office, George Fox nudged a button on his desk. There were quite a few buttons on the console and several of them were marked in red. The one he touched now was not.

'Stand by, Shermin.' He turned his mouth toward an intercom pickup. 'Brayton? In here, please.' Back to the phone again. 'Let me make sure I understand exactly what you're telling me, Shermin. This meteor, or whatever it is, appears to be hollow.'

'Not "appears to be," *is* hollow. There's no question about that, sir.'

Fox didn't look up as Brayton entered. His assistant waited patiently, eyeing his boss with undisguised curiosity.

'Okay, *is* hollow. Any idea what that means?'

'I can think of several possibilities, sir.'

'Among other things it's an automatic affirmative two-oh-four. That puts the country, at least as far as this department is concerned, on a stage-one alert. You understand?'

'Yes sir. I've read my briefing books.'

'You'd be surprised how many consultants never even bother to pick the damn things up, let alone read any of 'em. I don't have to go into detail about what's at stake here, then. Keep me informed, and be damned sure of any conclusions you reach, Mark. Damned sure. I'm going to have to rely on your expertise in this matter, and you know it. So double-check everything before you make any final decisions. We go off half-cocked on this we could all end up with our balls in the bouillon.'

'I understand, sir.'

'It's good that you do. I know I can rely on you, Mark.' He hung up, considered his next move.

'What's up, chief?'

Fox gave his assistant the jaundiced eye. 'Either Shermin's

brain has imploded or else we're sitting on a possible two-oh-four affirmative.'

Brayton swallowed hard. 'No shit? I thought that part of the bible was in there for amusement value.'

'It's no gag. Not this time. Better upgrade the alert to stage two. Cancel the rest of my appointments for the day and get me some transportation. I'm going on a little trip, and not for my health.'

Brayton looked stunned. 'Declaring a two-oh-four is pretty big stuff, chief. A lot of people are going to want to know the reason why.'

'Keep it within the department as much as possible.' Fox rose from his chair and started around the desk. 'Tell anyone who gets persistent that it might have something to do with some harmless but potentially interesting Soviet space-junk. That's what I thought this was, so there's no reason why any nosy-bodies won't think the same. And for God's sake keep the Press out of it. We don't want them poking around until we know for sure what this is all about.'

Brayton nodded and turned to leave when a sudden thought made him turn back to his boss. 'What *is* it all about, sir?'

Fox was hunting through a file cabinet drawer. 'We don't know yet. So far we've nothing but possibilities. You'll know as soon as I know, and me, I'll know as soon as Mark Shermin does.'

The two men exchanged a meaningful glance and then went their separate ways. There was much to do, and not all of it pleasant.

Jenny looked over at her passenger. He seemed to have relaxed a little. Instead of staring straight ahead, he was starting to let his gaze roam lazily through the forest, the flowers growing on the highway shoulder, taking everything in. The gun rested in his lap again. Maybe it was too uncomfortable to keep stashed in his belt. Or maybe he just wanted to be able to get to it that much quicker.

She found she was starting to tremble again and forced

57

herself to clamp down hard on the wheel. 'Do you have to keep that thing in your lap like that all the time?'

He turned his attention away from the trees and back to her. 'Something is wrong?'

'You bet something is wrong.' She nodded toward the automatic. 'Those things, guns, make me a little bit jumpy.'

'Define "little bit jumpy."'

'Well, a little bit's like,' she held up thumb and forefinger, keeping the ends slightly apart, 'that's a little bit. Small, not much of anything. And jumpy's like nervous, afraid.'

'Afraid, yes.'

'You know that word?' She couldn't recall his having used it in her presence. 'Afraid?'

'Yes. I know.'

'How much English do you understand? You know more than you've said, don't you?'

'I am learning as I listen to you, and to your communicator.' He nodded at the radio, currently silent. 'I understand greetings in fifty-four local languages. I understand more English language – little bit. I learn more.' He went quiet again. After several minutes he leaned forward and popped open the glove compartment door. Seeing that it was crammed full of interesting material, he put the gun aside, by his right hip and well out of Jenny's reach, and began rummaging through the compartment's contents.

She watched him curiously. He appeared fascinated by the simplest everyday objects. 'Nothing much in there.' He extracted a small leather wallet. 'That's mine. Wallet.' She reminded herself that he didn't appear to be interested in thievery. Oh no, not at all. All he was stealing was the car – and her.

He opened the wallet and examined the few bills. Then he started flipping through the plastic sleeves, pausing at the second one.

'That's my driver's license,' she told him. 'You need one of those in order to be allowed to drive a car. That's my picture on it, and my name, Jenny Hayden.'

He spared her a single emotionless glance just to let her

58

know he heard, finished looking through the wallet. He replaced it in the glove compartment and resumed his foraging. Jenny watched him for a while longer and discovered she was more bored than anxious. The road was a more animated companion than her passenger.

She stood the silence for a half hour before asking, 'Look, what do you want, anyway?'

He looked up from his work. Her small penlite flashlight lay disassembled on his lap. 'I want to go to Arizona-maybe.'

'No, I don't mean now. What I meant was, why did you come here? To this place. To my world.'

He put the flashlight back together before replying. 'I come – to see inhabitants of planet Earth.' He put the light back into the glove compartment, swapping it for a bottle opener fashioned in the shape of a frog.

'You mean you're like, sort of an explorer? You're just looking around?'

'Looking around. Yes. I observe, study, have contacts maybe. Learn.' He traded the bottle opener for an old baseball cap, immediately recognizing it from the home movies he'd watched the night before. He turned the battered piece of material over in his hands. Jenny kept her gaze glued to the highway ahead.

'I see. And, uh, when you go back to wherever it is you came from will you be taking any, uh—' She turned to him, wanting to finish the question but dreading the possible answers.

What she saw made her forget everything else.

'Oh my God.'

The visitor had donned the baseball cap. Now he was grimacing at her with a passable copy of Scott's sly smile. Even the angle of the cap on his head ws exactly the same as it had been in the movies. She continued gaping at him until the right front wheel complained and she wrenched the Mustang back onto the pavement. Gravel went flying, ticked against the window. She didn't care if she'd nicked the paint. She didn't care about anything else except the impossible vision from the immediate past which sat on the

59

seat next to her. She was starting to sweat.

The starman – might as well call him that as anything else, she thought wildly – looked pleased with himself. 'I look like – Scott?'

She had the Mustang under control again, which was more than she could say for herself. She inhaled deeply several times before she trusted herself to speak rationally.

'Yeah, you do – I guess.' Something caused her to frown and stare more closely at him. 'At first you do, anyway. But not really. Not if you look hard. Your nose is different because it's straight. He broke his twice. And there's something else, I dunno, something spooky about your eyes.'

'Define "spooky."'

That much was easy. 'Spooky is what you are. *You're* spooky.' She glanced back at the road, chewed on her lower lip. 'I saw you last night, in there on the living-room floor. You know. Flopping around, growing. Turning from a baby into a boy into a man.' She was amazed at the sound of her own voice. How calm she was, how quiet. How controlled. Easier to relate to the impossible from a distance, she thought.

'Tell me something. Could you have made yourself into anything you wanted? Like a dog or a bird?'

He nodded. 'If duplicatable material of sufficient quality available, yes.' He was watching her now, not the woods, not the road ahead. Watching for her reactions.

'Then why be what you are? Why do you want to look like Scott?'

'Difficult to explain. I have not enough right words yet. I want to look like Scott because I see you in images last night with Scott. I want you not be little bit jumpy. You not little bit jumpy in pictures with Scott.'

She stared at him, then reached down to switch on the radio. She needed to mull that one over, because it implied a great deal. Among other things, it suggested that he was concerned about her state of mind. Well, he had company on that one. But it wasn't the sort of reaction you'd expect from someone who meant you ill.

The radio picked up an oldie but goodies station. That was fine with her. The last thing she wanted to listen to just then was the news.

Bing Crosby was crooning at her from out of a simpler, more comprehensible past. Good old Bing. The song was familiar: 'and would you like to swing on a star, carry moonbeams . . .'

Uh-oh, wrong lyrics. Hastily she leaned over to punch up another station.

The hangar reminded Shermin of a football stadium on a Thursday morning: vast, empty, and quiet. Within its cool high depths the S-76 looked like a nesting sparrow on the West Texas plains. Not that it was devoid of activity. He strode briskly toward the center of the hangar. Uniformed technicians were hard at work there, moving equipment into place, uncrating electronics, setting up and testing instruments. Within the hangar, a complete chemical and physics laboratory was being erected.

Resting nearer the back was the meteor, or whatever it was. It was already surrounded by sophisticated electronics. More were being cabled together and set in place as he drew close. By the end of the day the entire setup would be on-line and ready to go.

Three men were hard at work atop the meteor. He recognized Bell and two technicians who had taken the place of the two airmen from the impact site. They'd drilled a larger hole in the top of the object and were trying to create a wider gap by using a hydraulic jack on the opening.

Despite being well anchored the jack was showing a disconcerting, not to say dangerous, tendency to jump all over the place. Bell was sweating profusely and wore the look of someone trying to facet a hundred-carat diamond with a jackhammer.

Another figure came up behind Shermin, drawing his attention. He recognized the radioman from his chopper.

'Hi.' Lemon looked past him, toward the meteor. 'What

61

are those guys trying to do?'

'Doing the best they can, Lemon.'

The radioman made a face. 'You're just a regular fountain of information, aren't you, Mister Shermin?'

He grinned apologetically. 'Sorry. In my field volubility's considered something of a drawback.'

'Yeah, whatever.'

Shermin nodded toward the sheet of paper Lemon held. 'Something for me, Lemon?'

'What?' The radioman forced himself to tear his attention away from what was going on atop the meteor. 'Oh, yeah. I remembered what you told me about police calls. You *did* say you wanted to hear about anything weird, out of the ordinary?'

Shermin nodded. 'Anything.'

'Yeah, well, I don't know that it's worth much, but since you didn't exactly give me specific guidelines I figured I might as well use my own judgment.' He looked down at the paper. 'I got this one off the general channel the cops around here use. Just picked it up from Ashland.'

'Where's that?'

Lemon waved southward. 'Out there somewhere. Small-town country. Me, I miss New York, but that's neither here nor there.'

'Yes, it is. It's there.'

Lemon didn't smile. Shermin was okay, for a government operative, but something of a wise-ass. 'It happened sometime this morning. What the report was about. Seems a guy named Heinmuller,' he checked the sheet again, 'Brad Heinmuller, had a collision with a hopped-up seventy-seven green Mustang.'

Shermin shrugged. 'That doesn't qualify as out of the ordinary.'

'Gimme a chance to finish, will you? Seems the gal who was driving the Mustang jumped out of her car after the collision and started running toward Heinmuller shouting that she was being kidnapped. But when he went to help her, the guy who was with her, the kidnapper candidate,

62

just kept yelling "greetings" over and over. Then he melted Heinmuller's lug wrench.'

Shermin got very quiet for a long moment. Finally he said carefully, 'He yelled "greetings" and melted his lug wrench?'

The radioman nodded. 'Hey, weird you want, weird you get. Does it mean anything?'

'I don't know. You heard the report. You're sure about the details?'

'Yes sir. You think I could make anything like that up?'

'No, no. Tell me something, Lemon. How do you melt somebody's lug wrench?'

'It wasn't exactly an in-depth report.' He handed Shermin the printout. 'This is a hard copy transcribed straight from the report. I taped it too, if you want to hear it.'

'No, that's all right.'

'You got it all, Mister Shermin. Me, I just copy 'em down. I don't explain 'em. Isn't that your job?'

Shermin politely ignored the question, inquired, 'I don't suppose anybody got a license number?'

'Give this Heinmuller credit; if he's a nut, he's an observant one.' Lemon indicated the printout. 'It's right there, down near the bottom of the page. Wisconsin plates, PXV two-three-seven. I'm checking the owner through the DMV in Madison.'

'That's very thoughtful of you, Lemon.'

Again the radioman looked uncertain. 'Mister Shermin, I'd sure like to know what all this is about.' He tapped the transcript. 'I feel mighty peculiar treating stuff like this seriously.'

'Don't let it get to you. We're all feeling a little funny about this whole business just now. Maybe I'll be able to tell you a little more about what's going on here when I've been able to figure it out myself.'

He was interrupted by a loud, metallic *crack*. Both men turned to look at the meteor. Bell was peering downward. He stared for a long moment, then seemed to shake himself awake. He looked over and gestured silently for Shermin to join him.

'Excuse me,' he told Lemon.

'Yeah, right.' The radioman watched as he jogged toward the object, trying to connect it to the police report he'd just handed over and failing utterly. Well, the world was full of crazy fools, as his mother never tired of telling him. He turned and started toward the exit, anxious to return to the sanity of his chopper.

Shermin went up the scaffolding that had been erected around the meteor and stepped out onto the cool, unyielding surface. Well, not entirely unyielding. The jack had bent back the flange Bell and his men were using until the black exterior had given way. He found himself staring down at a triangular opening that measured maybe a yard across each leg. He bent over and sniffed. No odor. Kneeling, he ran his fingers around the inside edge of the opening, then reached deeper and bent his arm so he could feel of the interior lining. It was smooth to the touch. Bell and the two technicians watched silently.

He sat down and put his legs through the hole. It would be tight but he thought he could squeeze through. 'I'm going down,' he told the major. 'I have to, you know.'

Bell nodded somberly. Behind him, one of the techs was leaning forward, straining to see inside. 'I know. Just watch yourself, okay? It might be booby-trapped or something, especially if it's Soviet.'

'If it's Soviet I'll carry it all the way to Washington on my back. As for booby traps, you saw how it "landed,"' Shermin reminded him. 'Not what I'd call a gentle touchdown. Whatever this thing is, it's banged up pretty good.' He took a deep breath, put both hands on the sides of the opening, and lowered himself inside.

It wasn't far to the bottom. Overhead he could hear Bell yelling, 'Someone get some lights up here!' A moment later the dark interior of the meteor was bathed in the glare of a powerful floodlight and Shermin could see his surroundings clearly.

He leaned forward and cautiously ran his fingers over what appeared to be crystalline projections. At first sight

64

he'd thought they were natural and growing from the inside wall. Now that he was close he could see them for what they really were, artificial attachments to the object's interior. They varied greatly in size and shape. Patterns lying within the translucent material suggested the same kinds of inclusions that were found naturally in quartz and other minerals, save that they were far too symmetrical and complex to have formed by chance. They had been built.

Bell leaned over the opening and yelled down at him. 'You okay in there, Shermin?'

'What?' He was mesmerized by the sights surrounding him. He recalled the words of archeologist Howard Carter who, when he'd first stumbled into Tutankhamun's tomb, could only stammer to those who asked him what he was seeing, 'Wonderful things.'

'Yeah, I'm okay.'

'What the hell is it?'

This time Shermin couldn't answer. He was too busy. Turning away from the crystal wall – he tried to think of it as something other than a control station and could not – he bumped something on the floor with his left foot. The projection moved and a small panel of metallic glass slid silently aside, revealing the interior of a beautifully fashioned metal box. The interior showed seven small, round indentations where small egg-shaped objects might once have been stored. He picked up the container, examined the exquisite craftmanship briefly, and then passed it up through the opening to the major. He in turn handed it over to one of the technicians, who bore it away toward the makeshift lab as if he were carrying the jewels of the moguls.

A larger, dark-colored object lay beneath a panel in the floor. Bell looked past him from above.

'What's that thing? It looks like a gold record.' He laughed nervously. 'Maybe this gadget you're exploring belongs to some singing star somewhere.'

Shermin didn't laugh as he bent over to study the disk of anodized metal. 'It's a record all right, Major, but you couldn't play it back on your stereo.' He ran his fingers over

65

the transparent facing protecting the disk. The panel slid back, allowing him to remove the pitted piece of metal. It was cold and slick and he trembled with the thought of where it must have been.

'It's sort of an invitation,' he reminded Bell. 'Do you recall the packages we sent out with the Voyager probes? Included with each was a gold anodized disk containing about a hundred pictures of typical Earth scenes encoded on the audio spectrum, along with greetings in a host of languages topped off with a nice little speech from Kurt Waldheim.'

'Kurt who?'

'He was secretary-general of the United Nations at the time. His talk was kind of along the lines of "ya'll come over and see us sometime."'

Bell was staring at the disk. 'It could be a fake, a copy. This whole setup could be a ploy of some kind, designed to get us all worked up over nothing. I wouldn't put it past our Soviet friends to concoct something like this just to devil us.'

'If that's what they'd like then they've partly succeeded,' Shermin replied, 'because I'm sure as hell all worked up. But I don't think this thing is Soviet in origin.' He ran his fingers lovingly over the peculiar instruments, the strange glassy substance that lined the interior. 'There's stuff in here that doesn't look like anything I've ever seen before. I don't think anyone's ever seen stuff like this before.'

'But you can't be positive it isn't Soviet?'

The military mind, Shermin thought tiredly. And he liked Bell, too. 'Not until the lab boys run some tests on this stuff, no.' He smiled, aware no one could see him. He was smiling for his own pleasure, and it was an odd sort of smile. 'Just one thing. When they get to work in here, tell them to be sure not to use any lug wrenches.'

Up above, one of the technicians turned to whisper to Bell. 'Now what the hell's that supposed to mean?'

Bell whispered back to him. 'He's from Washington.'

The technician nodded, as if that explained everything. 'Oh.'

*   *   *

Jenny looked absently over at her passenger. He was holding two of those funny little gray spheres in his right hand, manipulating them methodically without looking at what he was doing. It reminded her of the courtroom scene from *The Caine Mutiny*, with Humphrey Bogart as the psychotic Captain Queeg endlessly tumbling the ball bearings through his fingers. It wasn't a reassuring comparison. She nodded toward them.

'What are those for?'

'Different things,' he replied uninformatively.

'That's nice to know.' Her sarcasm was lost on him and she was too bored to press the matter further. Her eyes drifted to the dashboard and she noticed the lagging needle on the fuel gauge.

'We're going to need gas.'

'Gas,' he repeated.

'For the car. Gas, fuel, energy.' She eased up on the accelerator. 'I step on the gas, the car goes. I take my foot off the gas pedal, the car stops. Understand?'

'No, I do not understand.' He appeared genuinely puzzled. 'How can car be out of energy so soon?'

'Check with Standard Oil. I'm just telling you.' She pointed toward the dash. 'That little window there is the gas gauge. When that needle drops down to "E," the big letter there, that means the tank's empty. No more gas. The car stops. Period.' She eyed him sideways. 'What do you want me to do?'

He thought a moment before replying briskly, 'Get gas.'

The sign in front of the cabin said it all briefly.

FOR SALE
GILMAN REALTORS – ASHLAND

Shermin slowed, checked his badly crumpled map, then turned off the access road and drove toward the house. He couldn't have gone much further anyway, not without ending up in the lake. And it was the only house at this end of the road.

There was a mailbox stuck on a rough-hewn post between the carport and the house proper. The name on the side confirmed his location: HAYDEN.

Another car squatted in the driveway. He pulled up and parked next to it. He admired the way the cabin fronted on the little bay and the lake beyond. There was a small dock and lots of trees and quiet. A long way from DC.

There was also no sign of a good deli, bookstore, newsstand, or computer terminal. Everything in its place, he told himself, and this wasn't his. Pretty, though. A sound made him turn back toward the house.

A pleasant-looking middle-aged woman was standing on the porch, holding a broom in one hand and staring back at him. She smiled pleasantly – something else different from back east – and gestured for him to approach.

'Hi there. I'm Mrs Gilman. Come right on in.'

'Thanks.' He climbed the couple of steps, noted that the wood was uncured but nicely finished. Love had been substituted for money in the course of the cabin's construction.

She followed him inside, closed the door behind them. There was a bucket and mop lying in one corner, and rolls of paper towels atop the breakfast bar.

'Excuse the mess. Jenny promised me that she'd clean it up, the poor thing, but I guess she couldn't handle it as well as she thought she could. I told her I didn't think her coming out here to pack up all by herself was a good idea, but she insisted, and she's hard to argue with. Stubborn, that girl. Anyways, I came out to check on her and when I saw the car gone and how things were going, well,' she smiled a motherly smile, 'I thought I'd pitch in and help a little. You know, surprise her.' She gazed at the jumble filling the living room.

'Try to see it without all the boxes and things. It would make a lovely hideaway for a bachelor. The nearest other cabin is quite a ways back off the road you came in on. You

68

have your own pier here and there's plenty of room in the carport for a boat as well as a car. Do you like to fish, mister, ah . . . ?'

Shermin was taking the room apart with his eyes, hunting for revealing details likely to escape the notice of a middle-aged real-estate lady. 'You said, "Jenny promised." That's Jennifer Hayden?'

'That's right. Poor thing. She's quite anxious to get rid of the place, you know. I told her that I thought she ought to be a little more patient, hang onto it a while longer, but I understand how she feels. So I told her that I'd do my best to get rid of it as quickly as possible, since that's what she wants. Two thousand down and she'd be willing to carry back a good-sized second.'

She didn't add anything further, aware that her visitor wasn't as interested in listening to her as he was in examining the cabin. He certainly was doing a thorough job of it, too, she mused. City fella by the looks and manner of him, badly in need of a place to get-away-from-it-all. It looked like she might have a sale despite the cabin's condition.

Her appraisal of Shermin was right on the mark, but he wasn't a potential customer.

He'd crossed the room to pick up a color eight-by-ten that had been resting atop a box of clothing. It showed a young man and woman standing in the snow. He showed the real-estate woman the picture.

'This is her? Jennifer Hayden?'

'Yes, it is.' Mrs Gilman frowned. An odd customer indeed. 'Why, is something . . . ?' A sudden thought made her switch in midsentence. 'You *are* here about the house, aren't you?'

Both of them turned toward the front door at the sound of another car pulling up outside. It came in fast and they could hear the gravel thrown as it skidded to a halt. It didn't go into the driveway but instead parked right out front. Doors opened and slammed shut in quick succession. Footsteps sounded on the steps leading up to the porch.

She moved to look out one window, glanced askance back at her silent, apparently unsurprised visitor. 'Something's wrong. Who are you? You're not here about the house, are you? What's going on here?'

The door burst open to admit a tall, husky blond man in a blue uniform. Insignia on his shirt identified him as a member of the Ashland police department. A chief's star decorated his hat.

'Howdy, Gretch,' he said to the woman. Then he caught sight of the quiet individual standing in the center of the room. 'You're the government fella they talked about? Shermin, wasn't it?'

'Right. Mark Shermin.' He put the picture back atop the box of clothing. 'And you're Chief Svarland, from Ashland?' The man nodded once. 'Thanks for coming out here.'

A bewildered Mrs Gilman looked from one to the other. 'What's going on? Has something happened to Jenny?'

'That's what we're trying to find out, Gretchen.' The chief jerked a thumb toward the door. 'C'mon in, Brad.'

Brad Heinmuller entered, brushed self-consciously at his hair. Shermin studied him closely. He didn't look like a nut, lug or otherwise. Svarland interrupted his examination.

'Just put out an All-Points Bulletin, Mister Shermin.'

That woke him up fast. 'An All-Points Bulletin?'

Svarland nodded, looked pleased with himself. 'Yep. Tristate. Don't worry, we'll nail 'em.' He indicated the tall, tired-looking young man standing nearby. 'This here's Brad Heinmuller. Fella who phoned in the report about Miss Hayden's maybe being kidnapped.'

'Kidnapped!' Mrs Gilman clutched her broom and looked ready to use it on somebody. 'I knew it. I knew something had to be wrong when I got here this morning and saw the packing and cleaning half finished.' She looked at Shermin. 'Didn't I tell you I thought something was wrong? Her car gone, the door unlocked, not even a note on the counter – and that bullet hole in the window.'

Svarland perked up. 'Bullet hole?'

Mrs Gilman moved away from the window. 'Why, yes.

70

k pulled up behind the station. The driver
of his rig and strode purposefully across the
rd the starman. He took in the silent waiter and
dies' room door and spoke sympathetically.
her out, hey?'

starman said somberly.

er nodded as he shoved open the mens' room
pped inside. 'I know how she feels. I just ate a
cashews between here and Madison. Man, let
don't ever eat a whole can of cashews at one
n't bother to shut the door behind him.

happened to look over his shoulder it was to
he'd spoken to staring in at him. The man
rucker turned his face away. Evidently he'd
both the guy's attitude and the reason for his
de the john.

. 'Every goddamn place you go,' the trucker
mself. Finishing his business, he zipped up
ck toward his idling truck. The starman
aside for him, grinned, and made the
ure.

' he said.

e trucker gave him the finger. 'Up yours,

watched interestedly as the trucker climbed
is rig, shoved it in gear, and rumbled back
hway. Somewhere off in the trees a bird
commentary on the eighteen-wheeler's

the starman repeated softly to himself,
s voice. Interesting. Words and phrases
interchangeable between individuals, but
quencies were distinctive. It was important
things. He jabbed a finger toward the still
bird and said, 'Up yours.' Satisfied, he
nself when the ladies' room door opened.
appeared slightly startled to see him still
ting on her.

rong?'

Right over here. See?'

Both men crossed to inspect the puncture and the glassy spiderweb that radiated from it.

'Old?' Shermin asked the chief. The older man ran one finger around the edge of the hole, finally shook his head.

'Too many splinters still around. It's new, Mister Shermin.' His tone was grim. Shermin could see him thinking, *not in my district*.

'I told you.' The real-estate lady looked vindicated. 'I would have noticed if it was here before. It's my business to notice things like that.'

Behind them, Heinmuller shifted uneasily from one foot to the other. 'Look chief, I want to help, but I've got a door to hang in Ashland and my boss ain't the understanding type, you know?'

Shermin turned away from the window. 'Sorry, Mister Heinmuller. We really do appreciate your cooperation. As for your boss, don't worry about him. If you have any trouble, just have him call the chief here and he'll explain what's going on.'

Heinmuller was only slightly mollified. 'You don't know my boss,' he said glumly.

'We won't keep you but a minute, I promise.' Shermin went back to the box and picked up the picture again. 'All I want to know is if you're positive the young lady in this picture is the same one you saw on the road this morning.' He handed over the eight-by-ten, waited anxiously for the young man's reaction.

He barely glanced at it, handed it back. 'Yeah, that's her. Hey, wait a minute, let me see that again.' Shermin passed it over. He squinted hard at the glossy, looking for something he might have missed. Heinmuller's next words surprised him anew.

'Yeah, I'm sure of it.'

'Sure of what?' Svarland pressed him.

Heinmuller tapped the photo. 'Him. This here fella in the picture is the same guy I saw out there wrestling with her.'

Mrs Gilman folded her arms and spoke with quiet

assurance. 'Well I don't know what's going on here, but that's one piece of nonsense I can put to rest. One thing's sure and that's that nobody saw that man this morning.'

'I'm telling you it was him.' Heinmuller was insistent. 'I'm as sure of him as I am of her.'

'Then there must be something seriously wrong with you, young man.' She indicated the picture. 'That's Jenny's husband, Scott Hayden. He was killed last April.'

It was a long way to the next town, so Jenny was relieved when the service station appeared around a turn in the road. The last thing she wanted was to be marooned out in the woods with this whatever-he-was with night coming on. Better to keep driving. At least that way she had some control over her surroundings. And she still might be able to work something when he wasn't ready. She knew the Mustang a lot better than he did.

If only he didn't know the forty-five so well.

'We're coming to a gas station.' She pointed up ahead. 'See? I'm going to stop and fill up. Okay?'

He nodded once. 'Okay.' Then he reached under the seat and brought out the gun, tucked it out of sight in the waistband of his chinos and pulled the front of his shirt out and over to cover it, exactly as he'd seen Scott do in the home movies.

She pulled into the station. There was only the one attendant, which was the norm for an isolated place like this. He was just giving change to someone driving a blue Buick. The customer grinned as he revved his engine and saluted the gas jockey with a jaunty thumbs-up.

'Take 'er easy, Phil.'

The attendant echoed the gesture as well as the words. 'Take it easy.' The Buick pulled out and Jenny took its place beside the pumps. The attendant gave her a pleasant smile.

'What'll it be today, folks?'

'Fill 'er up. Unleaded,' Jenny instructed him.

The starman leaned over and stared up at the young man, smiled politely. 'Gas.'

'Gotcha.' Whistling to hi[m] toward the pump.

Jenny looked at the star[m] started to get out. He eyed h[is] front of his shirt just enoug[h]

She tried to sound as cas[ual] know. But I've got to go to[...] shoot me for that, go ahea[d...] and she tried to explain. 'T[...] a person goes – when a pe[rson...] tiredly. 'The hell with it[...] stepped out and headed [...]

He watched until she'[d...] the car and stood inspec[ting...] was bright and warm, b[...]

It was the baseball c[ap...] had been worn by Sc[ott...] proper. Removing it[...] divining its intended [...] properly, front to ba[ck...] Eminently satisfied w[ith...] Jenny's path, hurryin[g...]

She was just open[ing...] moved in close behi[nd...]

She put up a han[d...] Turning, she indica[ted...] the word LADIES w[...] 'Ladies. Me. Wom[en...] only. Understand?[...]

When he didn'[t...] which had the a[...] figure.

'Men. You onl[y...] the other door ar[...] tal reasons Jenn[y...] further. She we[...]

As her com[...] doors while try[ing...]

sizable truc[k...] hopped out [...] asphalt tow[ard...] the locked l[...]

'Can't ge[t...] 'Gas,' the [...]

The truck[...] door and ste[pped...] whole can of [...] me warn you[...] time!' He di[d...]

So when h[e...] see the man [...] smiled. The t[...] misunderstoo[d...] presence outsi[de...]

Whattheh[ell...] muttered to h[imself...] and started ba[ck...] politely move[d...] thumbs-up ges[ture...]

'Take it easy[...] Growling, th[e...] buddy.'

The starman [...] into the cab of h[is...] out onto the hig[hway...] offered its own [...] departure.

'Take it easy, [...] practicing Scott['s...] were apparently [...] inflections and fre[...] to remember such [...] singing but unsee[n...] was nodding to hi[m...]

'Oh, hi.' Jenny [...] standing there wa[...] 'Something is w[...]

'No – nothing. I thought you'd have gone back to the car by now, is all.'

He shook his head. 'Nothing to learn in the car. Much to learn out here.'

'Yeah, well, come on. Let's go.'

Instead of turning with her, he stepped into the ladies' room.

Oh my God, Jenny whispered to herself. She paled and stood there praying silently that he'd come out quickly.

He did not. He took his time studying the bathroom, noting the slight differences between it and the tiny room marked MEN. In most respects the two rooms were identical. There was a john, basin, towel rack, and mirror. Taped to the mirror was a paper towel on which had been written in light pink nail polish, KIDNAPPED. GOING WEST ON 169 GREEN MUSTANG LIC. PXV 237 HELP.

There was also a broom in one corner, a small couch and a dispensing box on one wall. Having completed his examination he exited. 'Come on,' he told Jenny, 'let's go.'

She let out a long sigh and followed him back to the car.

The attendant was standing in front of the Mustang, putting the license number down on the purchase slip. She gave him her credit card and he ran it through the printer, then handed card and slip over. She signed the chit, conscious of alien eyes following every step of the procedure, accepted the receipt and card, and slid into the driver's seat.

He didn't say a word as she thanked the attendant, put the car in gear, and pulled out onto the empty highway. She pushed it up to sixty and found herself stifling a yawn.

'Don't you people ever get tired?' she asked him curiously. 'We've been going for hours now and you've hardly even blinked.'

'No. We do not get tired. And I have blinked.' He did so, as if to demonstrate that he could. 'Not from being tired. Analysis indicates periodic action is required for proper lubrication of visual receptors.'

'Sorry I asked.'

They drove along quietly for another ten minutes before he said quietly, 'Kidnapped?'

'What?' She turned to him as he removed a folded paper towel from his pocket and pointed to her desperate inscription.

'What is "kidnapped?"'

That was it. She just couldn't take this anymore. She'd handled it well up to now – hadn't she handled it well up to now? But everyone has their breaking point and she'd finally reached hers. Mentally and emotionally she was completely drained. She had no more reserves and in any event, she was just plain tired.

She crushed the brakes and brought the car to a skidding halt on the shoulder. More than anything else, she was surprised by the intensity of her voice.

'You wanna know what kidnapped is? All right, I'll tell you. It's being dragged out of your house in the middle of the night and being scared and dirty and hungry and going to the john in cruddy gas stations so if you're going to shoot me go right ahead because I'd rather be shot than scared to death every minute of the day and *I can't take it anymore*.' She turned away from him, dropped her head.

'Go on.' She swallowed. 'Get it over with.'

She found that she was trembling. She was too exhausted to scream.

Nothing happened.

When she finally spoke again, her tone was much subdued. 'Come on, what are you waiting for? Do it.'

There was a snicking sound. Something landed gently in her lap. Opening her eyes, she looked down to find herself staring at the clip from the automatic.

'I mean you no harm, Jennyhayden,' he told her softly. 'I do not want to hurt you.'

'You . . .' Suddenly she was crying. It was positively the last thing she wanted to do, the last thing she expected to do. She couldn't help it, couldn't stop the tears from flowing no matter how hard she tried. She didn't try very hard.

A hand reached over to gently squeeze her arm. Somehow that made it worse than ever.

Four

No one gave the green Mustang a second look as it cruised smoothly down the highway. There was nothing unusual about it, except perhaps its speed. It was travelling sixty miles an hour. That in itself was not extraordinary. What was remarkable was the precision with which it maintained that speed. It didn't matter whether it was going uphill, or down, or around the occasional curve. The speedometer needle clung to the small space between the six and the zero as if it had been glued there. No cruise control could have maintained that speed with such precision, and in any case, the Mustang was not so equipped.

But then, the mind that was monitoring the flow of fuel to the engine was far more accurate than anything electronic.

The radio had been bopping away until a series of particularly uninformative and annoying commercials replaced the music. The starman took one hand off the wheel and killed the radio.

New music replaced the commercial pitches. It emanated not from the radio but from the driver, from somewhere deep inside. It didn't sound quite like it was supposed to because the body that was producing the music wasn't designed to generate such sounds, but it was a reasonable approximation. The music was soft, atonal but without being harsh. Not twelve-tone fragments and not Cageish raucousness but something very different. Harmonious and yet constantly changing.

Jenny blinked and looked up. She was curled up in the passenger's seat and she'd been sound asleep. It took her a

77

moment to realize that the music had to be coming from the starman.

It produced a gentle warming inside her, a feeling of peace and vast relaxation. Whether the sensation was the product of the music or of something else he was putting out she didn't know. There was a sweetness to it, an innocence that was utterly different from the sounds he made when he spoke to her. Probably he found human speech harsh and rough, she thought. What must his own language sound like? His own voice?

He sensed the attention and stopped.

'I am sorry. I did not mean to disturb your rest. Just because we do not rest does not mean that I should interrupt yours. It was impolite of me. It will not happen again.'

'Don't worry about it.'

'But I did awaken you.'

'Sure you did, but it's okay. I – that was a nice song. Do they sing a lot where you come from?'

'Sing?' He considered the word, applied it to what he'd just been doing. 'Yes, we sing. This body,' and he touched his throat, 'is not right for our kind of singing. It is difficult, but the sounds are not so very different.'

She remembered the little bit of Mick Jagger he'd done for her back before she'd known what she was dealing with. 'What about eating? Don't you ever get hungry, either?'

'Hungry?'

'Empty. Here.' She touched her stomach. 'Like a car needs gas. Remember the gas station? Well, people here on this world, we need food as well as rest. Energy. Fuel. Understand?'

'Yes.' He nodded. 'We get energy differently. This body is strange, primitive. Oxydation of chemicals produces . . .'

'Spare me the chemistry lecture,' she said quickly, putting up a hand. 'Are you feeling that way? Empty? Hungry?'

Another nod. 'Yes. This body has a terrible emptiness. Different sensation than from when we need energy. This is called hungry?'

'That's it. And when people get hungry they have to eat.' She made eating motions with hands and mouth.

'Eat. Yes, we must do that. I can prevent this body from needing rest, but I see now the connection with eating. We will stop at food station. You have hungry too?'

She let out a relieved sigh. 'Are you kidding? Why do you think I brought it up? I'm starving. I haven't had a thing to eat since,' her eyes suddenly bulged and she gestured wildly ahead with both hands, 'my God, look out!'

There was a highway intersection in front of them. The light had turned from green to yellow and instead of slowing down, the starman was accelerating. The Mustang leaped toward the intersection.

'What are you doing?' she screamed at him. Because this time the intersection wasn't empty.

The tractor-trailer rig approaching from the right was racing toward Michigan at sixty-five and, since he had both the light and the right-of-way in his favor, the driver wasn't paying much attention to the intersecting lanes. He saw the Mustang rocketing toward him at the last possible instant, threw on his brakes and leaned hard on the air horn.

The howling rig jack-knifed without turning over. The Mustang scraped past the towering chrome grill, did a complete three-sixty on the rain-soaked pavement, and finished by pointing itself in the right direction. They'd gone through the intersection without suffering so much as a scratch.

Which was more than could be said for the cars that piled into the back end of the truck, not to mention each other. Horns and the sound of grinding metal filled the air.

The noise faded rapidly as the starman pushed the Mustang back up to sixty. Jenny sat next to him, breathing hard and fast. The starman was grinning back at her, looking at the world like a kid who'd just stepped out of an 'E' ticket ride at Disneyland.

'Okay?' he said.

'Okay?' She fought to get her breathing under control. 'Are you crazy? You almost got us killed back there! You said you'd been watching me, that you knew the rules. That's the only reason I agreed to let you do some of the driving.'

'I do know the rules.'

'Like hell you do! For your information, that was a yellow light back there. It was yellow before we got near the intersection.'

He nodded agreeably. 'I watched you very carefully, earlier. Red light, stop. Green light, go. Yellow light, go very fast.' He smiled confidently. 'I know the rules good.'

She hesitated. How could she explain? She could hardly tell him that she'd been trying to attract the attention of a small-town cop by running that intersection.

'That was a mistake on my part,' she finally told him. 'Yellow means slow down and get ready to stop. Okay?'

'Sure. Okay.' He sounded just the slightest bit puzzled by this sudden change in the rules.

'You better let me drive.'

'No.' He studied the road ahead and looked pleased with himself. 'I will drive. Okay, no problem. Take it easy.' He leaned back in the seat, looking as though he'd been driving all his life.

She hesitated, turned to look out the back window. There was no sign of the truck that had nearly run them down and no suggestion of pursuit. Probably the drivers were too busy exchanging the names of their respective insurance companies to bother chasing the vehicle which had precipitated the pile-up in the first place.

Speaking of which . . . 'I'm going to have a great time with my insurance guy when one of those people back there reports this car. I can hear it now. "Well, no sir, I wasn't driving at the time. It was this fellow from outer space. No sir, that's not near Madison. No sir, I don't believe he did have a valid Wisconsin driver's license at the time, but I figured if he could drive a flying saucer he ought to be able to handle a Mustang. Well, yes sir, he did run a yellow light, but that was my fault. I didn't explain about lights too well and I was a little scared at the time because he happens to . . ."'

She stopped there. She didn't know how he'd react to learning that the body he'd duplicated and was now inhabiting was the perfect double of her recently deceased husband. Probably she was worrying needlessly. He might not make anything of the information at all. He might not give a damn one way or another.

But she would. It mattered to her, and every time she let herself think about it it depressed the hell out of her. Since she was depressed enough by the situation she found herself in, she determined to try not to think about it anymore.

A small restaurant materialized off to their left. Still shaken by the near accident, she wasn't ready to face other people just yet.

'Is that a food station?' he inquired.

'Yes, but keep going. We can do better.'

And I'll have to do better, she told herself firmly, or I'm going to go off the deep end.

Fox mulled his advisor's words over in his mind, looking for the simple way out. There was always a simple way out, if you were patient enough to hunt for it. He was something of a master at finding quick, simple solutions to complex problems, but for the life of him he couldn't conceive of one now.

He consoled himself a little by noting that there were no precedents for what was facing them. George Fox was a tidy man. It was useful for a man in his position to be tidy. But there was nothing very tidy about the current situation. Not if Shermin was right. It rankled Fox that he couldn't see a tidy, easy way out. He'd always been able to see the easy way out.

When he finally replied to the information he'd just been given he spoke with forced patience. 'Do you seriously expect me to ring up the president of the United States and tell him that an alien has landed here, has assumed the identity and body of a dead house painter from Madison, Wisconsin, run off with his widow, and is presently out tooling around the countryside in a hopped-up green seventy-seven Mustang?'

Shermin was glad of the hangar's openness. In a small room Fox's presence could become overpowering. The spaciousness of the hangar limited the intimidation factor.

Besides which, he knew that he was right.

He also had the moral support of Dave Goldman, a colleague working silently nearby. It wasn't much. Not against Fox. But what else could he tell the director? Truth was truth, whether he liked it or not. Whether the president liked it or not.

But sometimes it took more than the obvious to convince men like Fox. So Shermin explained one more time.

'We have the following givens, sir.' As he talked he was leading Fox over to the table where Goldman was working. Pictures and reports were lined up neatly atop the plastic. 'That man, Scott Hayden, was killed last April. He died in a construction accident. He's dead and buried. That's easily verified. His co-workers witnessed the accident, and it's pretty hard to fake a morgue photograph, much less the opinions of the fifty or so eyewitnesses who viewed the embalmed body before the funeral. I could order the body exhumed, of course, but in my opinion that would constitute the most grievous sort of investigatory overkill.'

'All right,' said Fox curtly, 'I accept the fact that the original Scott Hayden is deceased.'

'He has no brothers,' Shermin went on, 'no look-alike cousins. We checked that out right away. Despite all that, at approximately six o'clock this morning . . .'

Fox waved a hand at nothing and turned away from the table. 'All right. We've been through all that. It's just that it takes a while to get used to dealing with the impossible. What I want to know now, what I'm asking you now is – how can it be?'

Goldman looked up from his work. 'Has to be some kind of cloning deal. The replication's too perfect to have been accomplished just from the viewing of pictures.' He assumed a school-masterly tone. 'You know about cloning? Replication of an entire organism from the DNA contained in a single cell?'

Fox glanced back at him. 'I keep up as best I can, Mister Goldman. Just don't get too technical on me.'

'We found some hairs from Scott Hayden's head,' Shermin reminded his boss. 'They'd been kept in a photo album next to a picture of him as a boy. The plastic container had been opened and the individual hairs were scattered across the floor, as if they might have been dropped by someone working in a hurry.'

Fox still had a hard time accepting. 'Is that possible? To clone a living organism from the hair of a dead man? When it's removed from the body, doesn't the hair die?'

Shermin took a deep breath. 'Well, human hair consists of keratinzed cells. The follicular activity is cyclic and involves hormones. Retention of the genetic code by the cells in hair and fingernails is better than it would be in the softer tissues of the body. Remember that only one complete cell is required. Given the millions of available cells in a single strand of hair and sufficiently advanced techniques, theoretically the genetic code could be reproduced.

'As far as actual duplication of the complete, living structure, I can't imagine how that could be done, even with sequential photographs for a guide. The speed at which cell growth would have to take place would be a necessary function of . . .'

'I asked you a simple question,' Fox growled interrupting. 'Is it possible to clone a living body from the hair of a dead man?'

'For us? Given our present state of recombinant DNA technology, no. We can't even begin to imagine the requisite techniques, let alone postulate a workable procedure.'

'Then what the hell are we talking about? Magic?'

Goldman allowed himself a slight smile. 'You know, Mister Fox, the line between science and magic is pretty thin. I once saw an equation that measured magic as a function of time. Putting it another way, if you'd shown up in fifteenth century Paris with that calculator watch on your wrist and a flashlight in your pocket, you'd probably have been condemned to the stake as a warlock instead of being hailed as a master of some unfamiliar science.

'What we have here is a technology that's probably a hundred thousand years ahead of us. That's a conservative guess. We're the ancients, Mister Fox. The primitives, the Neanderthals. We're standing around gaping at the flashlight and wondering where the light comes from. Could you see yourself trying to explain the workings of a flashlight to an Egyptian pharaoh? You could talk yourself hoarse without ever convincing him it was anything other than a mystic manifestation of the god Ra.

'We're just barely advanced enough to realize how primitive we are.'

'Ancients.' Fox clearly found the idea disturbing.

'Technologically, anyway. We've just begun to understand how the universe works. We're still in kindergarten and suddenly there's a university professor among us. Two hundred years ago if you wanted to go from New York to Philadelphia you got a horse or booked passage in a carriage, right? Average speed, say, six miles an hour. A hundred years later you got on a railway train. Sixty miles an hour. Today you get on a jumbo jet that goes six hundred, and shuttle crews orbit the Earth at eighteen thousand.

'That's what we've done in two hundred years. Two long lifespans. Try to imagine what our technology will be like in a thousand years, or in a hundred thousand.'

'Assuming we're still around,' Shermin put in.

Goldman grinned at him. 'I was talking about our technological maturation. Emotionally, we're lagging way behind.'

Fox was subdued. 'Given everything you've said, I still have problems with this. What about his knowledge of everyday English, for example? He spoke to this guy Heinmuller out loud. No telepathy, no hypnotism. Plain old English.'

Shermin escorted him over to another bench. On top was a complex looking setup that resembled an audiophile's dream. Inside one box of black metal was a single golden disk.

Fox frowned. 'What's this? Top forty?'

'Something like that, only on an interstellar scale. Remember the gold information disks that went with the Voyagers?'

'Oh.' He shook his head. 'I remember all the yelling and screaming because it showed a nude man and woman.' He leaned over to study the player. 'This is a copy?'

Shermin smiled. 'One of the originals.' Turning, he gestured toward the meteor that had been revealed as a spacecraft. 'It was in there. Not stamped "return to sender," but you get the idea. Ever listen to the contents of one of these?'

'Not my department. I remember reading about it in briefings, but they didn't go into detail. What's it like?'

'Touch the second button from the top.'

Fox did so. Speakers began to hum. Silence gave way to soft violin music. Fox listened thoughtfully.

'A lot of people contributed to the recording,' Shermin mused aloud. 'I was one of those who helped put the final package together.'

Fox's eyebrows rose. 'You never told me that, Mark.'

He shrugged. 'My contribution was small. I was a collator, not a creator. It's not the sort of thing that comes up in general conversation at cocktail parties. Go back and reread my resume. It's in there.' He nodded toward the softly humming player.

'The package was designed so that any species intelligent enough to recover it and decipher its contents would be able to pick up a working knowledge of basic English, along with a few words of this and that in half a hundred other languages. I would've opted to include more English and less of the peripheral terran tongues, but the final decision on what to include was as much political as scientific. So anyone decoding the English therein would obtain a rough idea of syntax and a few hundred words and that's all. There's not enough in there to enable a listener to gain fluency.'

'This guy seems to be making himself understood.'

'So does Clint Eastwood, and he doesn't talk much either. He's learning, every day, sir. It's quite an achievement, when you think about it. He's not only employing an alien language, his own means of communication may consist of something entirely different from modulated sound waves. We've no idea, remember, of what his real body is like.'

'When he duplicated this Scott Hayden,' Fox asked, 'how come he didn't duplicate his memories as well as his brain?'

'Memories consist of stored series of electric impulses. They're not part of the genetic code. He could duplicate Scott Hayden's brain, but not his experiences.'

'Have you any idea,' Goldman suddenly broke in, 'what it would mean to talk to a being from a civilization like that? If their moral and aesthetic development advanced on a par with the technological, think of what we could learn from . . .'

He broke off as the music ceased and a new voice addressed them from the speakers.

'As the secretary-general of the United Nations, an organization of one hundred and forty-seven member nations who represent nearly all of the human inhabitants of the planet Earth, I send greetings. . . .'

'Greetings.' Shermin reached over to nudge the mute control, shutting out the rest of Waldheim's speech. 'That's what he said to Heinmuller out there on the road. I don't see what you're so concerned about.'

'Because that's also what the cannibal said to the missionary just before he ate him.'

'The question in this case,' Shermin said deliberately, 'is: who is the missionary and who are the cannibals? Remember, we shot at his ship, he didn't shoot at us.'

'We didn't know it was a ship, and the directives concerning unauthorized intrusions into US air space are pretty straightforward. Particularly when the intruder is of

86

an unfamiliar type and likes to go flying over nuclear submarine bases.'

'Paranoia,' muttered Goldman.

Fox turned on him sharply. 'Is it? Whatever you want to call it, it's my business and I'm charged with seeing that it doesn't threaten the security of this country. Why don't you ask this Jenny Hayden if I'm being paranoid?' Goldman didn't have a ready reply for that one. The matter of Jenny Hayden's possible abduction had been giving him and Shermin a lot of trouble.

Fox took the mute off the player and ran through the fast-forward. Snatches of greetings in many different languages ran together in a rapid-fire, meaningless babble. Finally they gave way to more music. Symphonic at first, then ethnic, then Mick Jagger rasping out, 'I can't get no, sat-is-fac-tion.'

Fox shook his head dubiously. 'I can't believe that grown men actually sent this crap into space.'

The late afternoon sun was bright as it shone through the Mustang's windshield, but it no longer troubled the starman. Not with the bill of the baseball cap pulled down low to shield his eyes. It was tugged down almost too far, but he needed all the help he could get. He had yet to get used to the spectrum of the local sun, even though he was viewing his surroundings through eyes engineered to make use of it. For one thing, the atmosphere was full of water vapor that played tricks with the fading light.

Jenny had been thinking quietly for some time. Now she looked over at him. 'I was wondering: you've pretty much got the hang of driving down, and if you meant it about not wanting to, you know, take me up there with you, then why don't you just let me out? You could take the car and a credit card and I could . . .'

'No!' Aware he'd spoken with unwarranted harshness, he hastened to soften his tone. 'You look for food station, please.'

'Yeah. Okay.' Disappointed, she settled back in her seat.

The road veered due west, leading them straight into the orange ball of the setting sun. She watched as the starman squinted tighter and tighter, until tears began to trickle down his cheeks. He must know so much about other things, things I can't even imagine, she thought, but here he's like a fish out of water. Not to mention his present body.

She reached over to lower the sun visor. Relief was immediate. He studied it for a second, then turned to her. 'Thank you.'

'Don't mention it. Listen, when do you have to be there?'

'What?'

'Arizona. Where you're meeting your friends. Is there some special time you have to be there by?'

'I will explain.' He nodded forward. 'You see this little star ahead of us?'

She peered hard through the windshield, but the sun was still too high for anything else to be out. 'What little star? Where?'

He pointed this time, at the setting sun. 'You must see it. You see it every day. That little star, there.'

'That's not a star. We call that the sun.'

'Call it what you like. It is a star. A very small one. Of no cosmological importance. Except to you, of course.' He hunted around on the floor until he located a crumpled piece of paper. 'Do you remember showing me this before?'

She recognized the road atlas. 'So?'

'You called this a map. There are other kinds of maps. Maps of stars. Your map shows big cities, little cities. Other maps show important stars, small stars.' Again he nodded forward. 'Very small star. Isolated. Away from the center. Not important.'

'Well, we like it,' she mumbled, abashed.

He considered her reaction. 'I do not say this to make you feel bad. My star is not big either. Facts are not designed to make anyone feel bad. They are for explaining.' He reached over to pat her knee, copying a gesture he'd observed another couple executing. 'When this little – when the sun appears,' and he jerked a thumb back over his shoulder, 'back there, three times more, I must be in Arizona-maybe.'

'It's just Arizona,' she corrected him absently. 'You're talking about daybreak. You have to be there at dawn, in two days?'

He nodded. 'Yes. No longer.'

'What happens if you don't make it? If you don't get there in time? Don't you have any leeway? Any extra time at all?'

'No. If I am not there at that time, they will go. My friends. They must. They strain the law by coming even this one time.'

'They'll go – without you?'

'Yes.'

'What will you do then?'

There was no expression on his face at all. 'Then the component chemicals which make up the being that is me will return again to the ever-changing brew of elements of which the universe is comprised.' She frowned at this and he added simply, 'I will die.'

'But why? Can't you stay here like you are, in that body?' She let her gaze rove over him, saw no sign of incipient disintegration, no hint of decay to come. 'You look healthy enough.'

'I am glad of that, but it is much easier to maintain outward appearances than interior functions. My continuing occupancy of this form is maintained partly by illusion, partly by constant effort. I am under a continual strain. It is painful and daily becomes more so. I can only live this way, inside this body, for a very short time. Soon after the third dawn I will lose my ability to keep it functioning, and it will fail as a mind-support system. I will be dead. Body will be dead, mind will die. Understand?'

She didn't reply. Not for the first time, he wondered what she must think of him. He turned his attention back to his driving.

'You look for food station,' he told her softly.

Another five minutes' drive brought them within sight of a sign. It was insistent, and a bit too big for the road.

'There's a place up ahead that looks good,' Jenny told him. 'Besides, it's getting late and I don't think I can go much further without something to eat, even if it's full of grease.'

'Emptiness inside,' the starman agreed.

She wondered if he was just talking about his stomach.

There were only a few cars in the lot when they pulled in. That did not necessarily imply criticism of the cuisine; they were a long ways from the nearest town. The terrain surrounding the restaurant was heavily forested, just like the country they'd been driving through for several hours now. Then too, it was not quite dusk. Early for fellow long-distance travelers to be stopping to eat.

One of the cars, a beat-up old sedan of indeterminate lineage, had a dead five-point buck strapped to the left front fender. The car's owner was locking his rifle in the trunk as they pulled in. Jenny watched him test the latch to make sure the trunk was secured before he turned and headed for the roadhouse door.

As they came around the sedan the starman had his first sight of the dead deer. Having no reason to expect anything abnormal, Jenny was startled when he slammed on the brakes.

'Whoa, take it easy, friend. The idea with brakes is to . . .' she broke off, seeing the expression on his face. It was twisted. Horror, fear and utter confusion were all mixed up together by someone who was uncertain of just how to manipulate his facial muscles to achieve the exact look he was seeking. There was nothing mysterious about the cause, however. He was staring at the dead animal as though hypnotized.

'What?' he finally managed to mumble.

'Deer. It's hunting season in this part of the country. Scott used to hunt, sometimes. We both liked venison. Fried tenderloin's about the best thing you can eat.' Memories

90

began to well up inside her once again. She forced them back down as she nodded toward the car. 'That's a dead deer.'

He considered this a moment. Then he carefully put the emergency brake on, removed the key from the ignition, and got out. Instead of moving toward the restaurant, he crossed in front of the Mustang and headed for the old sedan. Seeing this, the hunter paused at the cafe's entrance. His eyes narrowed as he saw the stranger approach his kill.

The starman stared at the corpse. The deer's tongue was hanging out and its eyes were still open. 'Dead deer. Why?'

Jenny came up behind him. 'I told you. People hunt them. To eat. For food, fuel.'

'Fuel. Our fuel is different. Do deer eat people?'

'Well, no, but . . .'

'Do people eat people?'

'Of course not. What do you think we are?'

'I think you are a primitive species that does not understand its place in the scheme of existence.' He gestured at the limp form lying across the fender. 'Beautiful life. Beautiful form and shape. Functional and beautiful. You destroy beauty. It is a mark of ignorance to destroy beauty. There are other ways of getting fuel.' Tenderly he reached out to caress the dead animal's flank.

That was enough for the hunter. He wasn't much of a philosopher, but in his book anti-hunting nuts ranked somewhere down there among commie pinkos and drug addicts. He moved quickly toward the parking lot. Never one to back away from a challenge, he knew one when he heard it. Damned conservationists were all over the place.

'What are you,' he asked the stranger, 'soft-hearted? Cry when you saw *Bambi*?' He stopped with his face only inches from the starman's.

'Define "*Bambi*."'

'Huh?' The hunter took a wary step backward. Anti-hunting fruits were one thing, but real looney tunes were something else again. He eyed the stranger the way one does an ace of diamonds in an opponent's hand that just happens

91

to have raspberry jam smeared on one corner.

Jenny tried to intercede. 'He doesn't understand,' she explained hastily. 'He's not from around here.'

'Oh, yeah? Then where's he come off criticizing an all-American pastime like hunting?' He stuck his face back into the starman's. 'No spikka da Inglish? Then hows about you keepa you mouth shut?'

Nonplussed by the proximity of this loud belligerent the starman retreated. Jenny grabbed his arm and gave the hunter her best apologetic smile. Then she steered her companion toward the beckoning cafe. For a moment she was afraid the man was going to challenge them again, but he stood guard over his deer and let them pass.

'Steer clear of these bozos,' she whispered to him.

Puzzled but anxious to please, the still confused starman asked plaintively, 'Define "bozos".'

'Don't look back, but that guy's one.'

The hunter followed them with his eyes until they vanished inside the cafe. His expression did not change, although he found his interest shifting from the critical stranger to the young woman holding onto his arm.

Five

It was getting dark outside the hangar as the three men walked toward the olive green army car. The driver quickly flipped his cigarette aside and stood to attention.

'Let me see if I've got this straight.' Fox spoke slowly for his own benefit, not that of his two companions. 'I damn well better have it straight because I'm going to have to tell it several times to some very important people. People who don't like ambiguous explanations.

'Both of you think – no, check that. Both of you are *convinced* that an alien has arrived here. In Wisconsin.' He shook his head in disbelief at that one, anticipating the response it would provoke back in Washington. 'And since arriving, he's cloned himself a human body. A body that it – we'll call it a he, since he's chosen a male body – can coexist with and manipulate in a humanlike manner.'

'That's about it, yes sir,' Shermin admitted.

Fox's gaze shifted to the other scientist. 'You concur, Goldman?'

'Completely. A number of extraordinary events have occurred here in quick succession, Mister Fox, and I don't have any other explanation for them. I'd like to find another one, believe me, but I can't. All the physical evidence underscores the validity of Mark's hypothesis, and that's not even taking Heinmuller's encounter into account.'

Fox sighed deeply. 'All right. I have to rely on your opinions. Heaven help you if you're wrong. Now, I think I can understand this business of physical replication, but how does the alien individual exist inside it? If he's inhabiting this duplicate of the late Scott Hayden, then what did he do with his own body?' He gestured with his head toward the massive hangar. 'We didn't find any

93

skeletons in that spacecraft – I think we can all stop referring to it as a "meteor."'

'In its original form the alien may not have needed a solid skeleton, sir,' Goldman told him. 'It may not normally make use of an inflexible frame as we know it. It might be an invetebrate form, like a mollusk.'

'It might be accustomed to living in a cloud of dense gas,' Shermin suggested, 'or in a concentrated magnetic field. It may be as far advanced in body as it apparently is in technology.'

'Wonderful,' Fox grumbled. 'I've heard about having to deal with a collection of ideas, but not literally.'

'Many think that a supercivilization will eventually develop a means for dispensing with much of what we consider necessary in the way of a physical envelope,' Shermin explained. 'That's all that a body is: an envelope, a package largely filled up with empty space and crude life-support systems.' He glanced at Goldman. 'Dave's right in guessing that it requires *some* kind of body to survive here. Otherwise it wouldn't have gone to the trouble of replicating Scott Hayden's.

'Perhaps its own body was damaged during the forced landing, or didn't survive long in our environment. The first thing a visitor to an alien world would need is a spacesuit. What better suit than the body of one of the dominant local life forms?

'As for the rest of the alien's "self," well, we're just starting to understand what the self is comprised of. Just for the sake of discussion, let's imagine that you could reduce everything that is someone to a sequence of electrical impulses. That's how we store information in computers. Think of a child's brain as a blank floppy disk, ready to be encoded with useful information. Under normal circumstances, information is imprinted on the human brain over a period of time, but theoretically one could receive a lifetime's knowledge in a few seconds, if we just knew how to make the transfer. Just like you'd transfer music from one tape to another.

'After the transfer's completed, you discard the old,

damaged tape and just play the new one. Same music in a new home. It's the music that's vital, not the tape. The tape's just a mechanism. So is a human body.'

'Crazy,' Fox muttered. 'I want a scientific explanation for what's going on and all I get from you two are metaphysics.'

'A rose by any other name,' Goldman put in. 'Crazy it is. Impossible it ain't. Not theoretically, anyway. Personally, I can see transferring thoughts and mental abilities from one mind to another a lot easier than I can conceive of cloning a new body from a single cell, and yet we have actual proof of the latter.

'What it boils down to, Mister Fox, is that we human beans have got us some company, wanted or not. That's reality, not metaphysics.'

'All right, you've convinced me. I don't know how much of this I really believe, but you're right about one thing; I haven't got a better explanation for what's happened here either. So what we're dealing with now is an alien superintellect in a cloned human body.' They'd reached the car. The driver came around to open the door. Fox hesitated before entering, glanced curiously back at Shermin.

'What we don't have yet is motivation. Any notion as to why we've got company just now? Any idea what a visitor like the one you two have described would want here?'

Shermin extracted a cigar from an inside jacket pocket and prepared to light up. The smoke would aggravate Fox, which was one of the scientist's favorite hobbies. He'd refined it to perfection the past couple of years. Sometimes Fox would protest and sometimes not. How strongly he reacted was a good clue as to how he was feeling about whatever subject happened to be under discussion at the time.

'I can think of any number of possibilities. Maybe he's an explorer, doing his field work. Only, the natives have up and interfered. Or maybe he's a tourist gone off the beaten galactic track in search of interesting snapshots to show the folks back home. But I kind of like the idea that he's here to check us over and see how we're doing in relation to a particular theorem derived from catastrophe theory.'

'Come again?' Fox asked.

'There's a hypothesis that says that once a civilization has reached our level of technology, it will do one of two things. Either it will get its collective act together and make peace among its constituent tribes, settle old differences, and then make the big jump out into deep space like grown-ups should, or else . . .'

'Or else what?'

'Or else it will muddle along like a bunch of spoiled brats until it blows itself all to hell.'

Fox nodded, then said politely but firmly, 'Excuse me, but would you mind not lighting that cigar until after I've left. You were saying?'

Shermin reluctantly put the cigar back in its pocket. 'I was saying that in so many words, maybe he's just come here to enjoy the fireworks.'

'Yes. Well, if that's all, then we don't have much to worry about. Nobody's going to blow anybody up. I have the assurance of the president on that.'

'Aplomb in the face of Armageddon.' Shermin shook his head wistfully. 'I wish I could be as cool about it as you, sir.'

'The world is not going to destroy itself.' Fox spoke with the conviction of a man soon to begin collecting his pension. 'Not if the IRS has anything to say about it.'

Shermin grinned at the sally in spite of himself. Fox could be a real bastard and then just when you thought you had him figured out, he could surprise you. He forced himself to get serious again.

'There is one thing that's been bothering me, sir. The local cops have put out an APB on our visitor. They've got him described as armed and extremely dangerous.'

'So?'

'Get it canceled. Some town whittler with a part-time badge in East Pisspot, Nebraska, could read that and blow him away before we've had our chance to meet with him.'

'I'd be glad to, Mark, except for one thing. Half the police force in the north central states have already been told that he's kidnapped a local woman. We got here too late to kill that story.

96

'If I put pressure on now to cancel the APB, the cops hereabouts are going to demand to know why. Right now this whole business is back page, one line local news. If I apply pressure to gag it, at least one cop is going to try to play hero by leaking it to the media. One always does. Word gets out that we're messing around with something a helluva lot more animated than a chunk of meteoric rock and all hell's going to break loose. We'll have the networks down on us from one side and Washington from the other. I can't risk that.'

'Can you risk having this alien killed before we've had a chance to talk with him?'

'If he wanted to talk to us all he'd have to do is walk into the nearest police station or federal building and turn himself in. We'd spirit him away from the local yokels soon enough.'

'Maybe he doesn't know it's that easy.'

'You're really rationalizing this thing's behavior, aren't you? Okay, if he doesn't know what to do, why doesn't he just ask the girl? If he wanted to make contact with the authorities, he's got someone to explain the proper procedures to him.'

Shermin looked away, into the night sky. 'I can't answer that one. Only she can.'

'Sure, that's right,' Fox said smoothly, 'and she can't answer our questions because it's pretty clear that, for whatever reason, he doesn't want her talking to anyone else. Otherwise he'd let her go. Wouldn't he?'

'I still think you ought to have that armed and dangerous bit canceled before we lose our first and only chance to date to contact an extraterrestrial civilization.'

'It's your job to find him before that can happen.' Fox got into the back seat of the car. The engine growled and Shermin stared as his boss was driven away into the fading light. He took out the cigar again, but this time eyed it distastefully and tossed it aside.

Goldman was sympathetic. 'Don't be too hard on him.'

'No harder than he deserves. No harder than his head.'

'He's only doing the job. You can't expect a senior

97

bureaucrat to see anything beyond his immediate personal concerns.'

'I know,' Shermin muttered. He kicked the cigar, watched it sail across the tarmac. 'That's what's so frustrating.'

The cafe was much bigger than it looked from the outside. It was an old building constructed of open woodwork. Animal heads were mounted on the big beam that supported the ceiling above the counter, alternating with pictures of the surrounding countryside. Up front was a smaller counter on which rested a cash register and a bowl of toothpicks. The case beneath the register contained a reservoir of ancient candy bars. An Elks' charity gumball machine stood in one corner.

In addition to the counter and the booths for diners there was a dance floor in the back, deserted now, and off to the left pool tables and a couple of old video games. Nothing separated the dance floor and the four-stool bar it fronted from the dining area.

The hunter who'd confronted the starman outside was engaged in a noisy and badly played game of eight-ball with his hunting buddies. A fair number of empty beer cans had already accumulated in their vicinity. Those opened but not yet sucked dry hung around like remoras waiting to attach themselves to their parent fish. In addition to the faint lament of country music from the region of the bar and the clack of pool balls smacking off one another there was a great deal of laughter brought about by coarse comments of the kind usually referred to by denizens of the lower depths as 'humor.'

From time to time the conversation would lapse while someone attempted a particularly difficult shot. The shot invariably missed, just as the deer killer's attention invariably wandered during such moments from the game into the dining room – and to Jenny.

What was a sassy little piece like her doing with a foreign nerd like that? He couldn't figure it.

Jenny sat on one side of the booth with the starman across from her. Spread out on the table between them was her

98

badly rumpled map of the United States. She was tracing a route through the mountain states with a red felt pen.

'From Denver – that's where we're near – it's south to Interstate 25. You pick up 1-40 westbound at Albuquerque and . . .'

She stopped when she saw that her companion wasn't paying attention. It was unusual for him to stray like that. He was looking out the window toward the parking lot and she didn't have to guess at what was drawing his attention away from her.

'Hey, forget the deer for a minute, okay? You can't do anything about it and I'm trying to show you something important. At least, you told me that it was important.' She tapped the map with the butt end of her marker. 'Now exactly where in Arizona are you supposed to meet your friends?'

The starman looked back down at the map. This time he studied it closely. 'A strange kind of map, Jennyhayden. It shows many of what you call roads, but few of the important things.'

'You've already told me that and I've already told you I can't do a thing about it. Complain to the Auto Club. It's all I've got.'

His finger moved over the paper, finally stopped at a place south of US 40 between the towns of Winslow and Flagstaff. Jenny leaned forward and frowned.

'Here? West of Winslow? I see a little speck on the map called Rimmy Jim's, but there's nothing south of that for a hundred miles except,' she looked back up at him. 'The big crater. Is that where they're going to meet you? Where that meteor hit millions of years ago? I read about that place in school.'

'Yes. It is the only place. You would not understand if I tried to tell you why it is the only place. It has to do with certain metals the meteor left behind in the ground when it struck and with,' he struggled with his rapidly improving but still unsteady English, 'lines of force that englobe your planet. My friends can only approach at certain places and certain times. On this continent this is the best place.' He placed his finger directly over the National Monument.

'Okay. That's empty country and this isn't summertime, so there shouldn't be a lot of tourists around. You shouldn't have any problem finding it by yourself if you have to. You sure you understand how to get there now?'

'Yes.' A pause, then, 'Why do you do this?'

'Better safe than sorry. I'm showing you in case something should happen to me. There's just one more thing. The credit card, for gasoline. You saw how that worked.'

She took her wallet out of her purse and fumbled through it, pulled out the card and muttered something under her breath as a half dozen other slips of this and that were pulled out with it. Typical of her wallet: jammed to overflowing with everything except money.

'Why should something happen to you?' The question was asked as if he was testing her for evidence of clairvoyance.

'Who knows? The way you drive, traveling with you could be detrimental to someone's health.' She essayed a forced grin and couldn't tell if he was buying her story or not.

He watched her for another moment before his attention dropped to the multitude of objects which had tumbled out onto the table. He reached down and picked one up before she thought to stop him. It was a photograph of two people, standing close together on a beach. Waves rolled behind them and the sun was just setting. He recognized Jenny and the man whose body he'd replicated.

She swallowed hard when she saw which picture he'd retrieved. 'That's me and Scott on our honeymoon. We went to San Diego. That's the Pacific Ocean behind us. I didn't think I'd ever see it in person – until I met Scott. He seemed to think you could get to see anyplace in the world if you just wanted to badly enough, and it didn't matter if you were rich or not. You just had to want to do it.' She saw the puzzlement on his face and tried to explain.

'"Honeymoon" is what we call it when two people first get married and they go off together and get to know each other and . . .' She swallowed again, but this time the lump in her throat refused to go away. A tear zigzagged a path down her cheek. She didn't pull away when he reached out

100

to touch it. Drawing his finger back, he studied the moisture thoughtfully.

'Salt water. What?'

'Tears.' She spoke sharply in spite of herself. Would he sense that her anger wasn't directed at him? That the renewed fury was born of frustration and aimed at whichever callous fates had decreed an early death for the kindest, sweetest man she'd ever . . .

Stop it, she ordered herself. The one thing she didn't want was to break down in a place like this, least of all in front of him. She didn't want to have to do any more explaining, because that would mean having to do some more remembering. She'd done altogether too much remembering these past few weeks.

'They're called tears,' she told him, once she had herself back under control. 'My husband, the man in the picture – Scott? He's dead. He's the one you're copy—' She broke off, sniffling, and tried again. 'We do that down here. Make tears. It's called crying. When somebody you love *dies* we cry about it.'

'Define "love."'

She tried to smile through her tears. 'You ask the simplest questions don't you? I don't know – it's like you care about somebody else more than you care about yourself, but it's more than that, too. It's *like* somebody is part of you and when they – when they die . . .' The words dissolved into soft sobs. She finally fished and found herself fumbling in her purse for a handkerchief, tissues, anything, only to have to use the table napkin. '*Shit*,' she muttered as she dabbed at her face.

'Define "shit."'

She choked on the unbidden laugh. 'Don't say that.' She tried to be serious. 'That's not a nice word.' Or maybe she imagined it. The waitress joined them, balancing their order on both arms.

'Shit,' the starman said emotio . . . and straighten her

Jenny was trying to dry . . . mind him, please. It's – expression at the same time. . .

he's a foreigner. He doesn't speak English too well yet.'

The waitress favored the starman with a jaundiced eye. 'Well, he's got a hell of a start on it. Who's the deviled egg on white toast?'

'He is.'

'Right. And a superburger, two orders of fries, two choc malts and two Dutch apple pie with whipped cream. Had a wedge of it myself at lunch – it's terrific. We've got a little old gal who makes them every morning, gets in here all by herself at six. Does everything by herself, won't let anybody else near the oven while she's baking and . . .' She saw the look on Jenny's face, smiled and backed off. 'Yeah, I know. I've got a nonstop mouth. Sorry. Enjoy.'

Jenny needed two hands to lift the hamburger and keep it together. It was overflowing with onions and pickle chips and juice. She was also just about hungry enough to eat an entire steer all by herself. She had to force herself to eat slowly. After two bites she noticed that the starman wasn't doing anything, just sitting there staring at his plate

'Well, go on, dig in, eat,' she told him. 'Fuel.' She took another bite out of the hamburger, felt the juice run down her chin and hurriedly found a clean napkin to wipe herself. The starman observed this silently, then used both hands to lift his wedge of pie and bite into it. It started to come apart in his fingers.

Jenny put her burger down quickly. 'Hey, wait – signals off. That's your dessert. You eat with a fork, not your fingers.' She demonstrated with her own utensil, then showed him his. 'That thing. Oh. And you eat it last. Sandwich first, dessert last.'

'Why?' He took another bite out the . . . . , Emily

She considered. 'Why? Who knows? What . . . . . Po . . . . . . a break, will you. Hey, what's the matter?' A strange ex . . . . sion had suddenly come over him.

'Dutch ap . . . .

other to try a pie?' He held it in one hand and used the . . . . p the filling from oozing out all over his hand.

'That's right. Y . . .

'It's terrific!' . . . e it?'

'See? For a primitive species we do have our good points.'
She took another bite out of the hamburger and followed it
with a swig of malt. He imitated her movements perfectly
with the pie and his own drink, even to leaving exactly the
same amount of malt around his lips.

The door swung inward. A bus driver entered trailing
several passengers in his wake. All of them headed for the
counter while the driver matter-of-factly addressed the room.

'Fifteen minutes. Anybody for Grand Island, Lincoln,
Omaha, or Chicago, the bus leaves in fifteen minutes.'

The passengers filled up the counter, ordering pie and
coffee and an occasional sandwich, while Jenny tried to
instruct her companion in the fine details of terran etiquette.
He had no trouble with the silverware because he ignored it,
eating with his fingers and explaining that he abhorred
duplication of effort.

He indicated the fingers of one hand, clutching the malt
with the other. 'Tools.' He nudged his knife and fork. 'More
tools. Duplication of effort. Why use twice as many tools as
you need to perform same task?'

'Well, because it's more polite that way.'

'Silly. Waste of energy.' He finished the last of the pie and
started in on the sandwich. 'No fork?'

'No. You eat a sandwich with your fingers, just like you're
doing.'

He considered this, finally shook his head sadly. 'I am
afraid I do not understand.'

Jenny wasn't sure she did either . . .

The passengers were starting to trickle back onto the bus.
The starman ignored them, producing loud sucking noises
as he drained the last bit of malt from the bottom of his glass.
Jenny had already finished. She sat quietly, watching him.

'Don't they have food like this up there?'

'We draw what we need from different sources. Energy,
fuel – difficult to describe in English.'

'You mean, like pills?'

'Difficult to describe. Not any taste like this, but make
you feel happy inside, all over.'

'Yeah, we've got some of those floating around down

here, too.' She rose. 'Excuse me. I've got to, ah, you remember?'

He nodded. She turned and headed toward the bar area, toward the little overhead sign and arrow that pointed toward the restrooms.

Before turning down the narrow corridor she looked back toward their table. He was still sitting there, staring out the window now, not even bothering to see which way she'd gone. For a moment she hesitated, reconsidered what she planned to do. Then she moved on. Not toward the pair of doors at the end of the narrow hallway, but through the big swinging one that led into the kitchen.

This meant she had to walk past the pool tables. Her passage drew several appreciative whistles and one mildly obscene gesture with a pool cue from the well-lubricated hunters. She ignored them utterly and didn't look around until she was safely inside the kitchen. The waitress who'd served them was waiting for an order-to-go, glanced over curiously at the intruder.

'Listen,' Jenny whispered anxiously, 'is there a back way out of here?'

The older woman considered a moment before replying. 'Yeah, sure. Through the back entrance and around through the parking lot. Why?'

Jenny didn't give her a direct answer. 'You know the guy I came in with? Well, I wonder if you'd mind giving him these – after the bus leaves.' She handed over a fistful of items. 'It's just a map, and some car keys, and a credit card.'

The waitress took them. 'You sure about this, honey?'

'I'm positive. He'll know what it's all about.'

'Yeah, I expect he will. Okay.' She shoved the stuff into one of her apron's copious pockets, picked up her order, and exited through the swinging door. She was back before Jenny was halfway to the service exit.

'I wouldn't go out the back right now, honey. That friend of yours? He's out there in the parking lot.'

'Oh no. Now what?' Mumbling to herself, she turned and rushed back into the dining room, having to run the same beer-sodden gauntlet of ribald remarks and envious eyes.

Sure enough, their table was deserted. She leaned over and peered out the window.

There he was, out in the middle of the poorly lit lot, standing next to the hunter's car. He was doing something to the dead deer strapped to the front fender. Well, if that kept him occupied, maybe she could find another way to sneak 'round to the waiting bus.

Her eyes suddenly widened and she pressed her face right up against the glass. The deer was moving.

Crazy. It was so crazy. She watched as it slid off the fender and tumbled to the pavement. The starman backed up, watching the animal closely. Shaking itself, the deer got to its feet. It stayed there for a long moment, scanning its surroundings as if orienting itself. Then it turned and trotted briskly off into the trees.

The deer's former owner had been staring at Jenny for as long as he could stand it. Now he sauntered up behind her to whisper into her ear. She smelled him at the same time she heard him.

"Scuse me, miss, but you strike me as a meat-eater. I could fix you up with a nice haunch of venison, and maybe a shot of pork to go with it if you . . .'

Her head snapped around and he saw the dazed look on her face. It was as if she hadn't heard a word of what he'd said. Frowning, he looked past her, out toward the lot.

'Son of a bitch!'

'Wait.' She reached for him. 'You don't understand. I don't understand either, but it's not like you think.'

'Like hell, lady! Let go of me!' He shook her off and stomped toward the doorway.

The starman was staring off into the woods where the deer had disappeared when the hunter grabbed him roughly by the shoulder and spun him around. 'All right, bright boy. What happened to the goddamn buck?'

'Buck? Define "buck."'

'The deer. My five-pointer, damn you.' Furious he gestured toward the now empty fender.

The starman turned and nodded toward the woods. 'He went away. There, into the trees.'

105

'Okay, comedian. We'll do this your way.' He feinted with his left. Instinctively the starman went with it, following the threatening lunge of the balled hand. That left him wide open for a hard right which sent him sprawling on the asphalt.

'Bingo.' The hunter looked pleased with himself.

His victim shook his head and tried to stand up. Four gray marbles fell out of his windbreaker.

'Still not feelin' talkative, boy?' the hunter growled. 'Okay. Let's try it one more time. What happened to the buck?' The starman ignored him as he turned to scramble after the precious spheres. A heavy boot slammed into his ribs, knocking the wind out of him and sending him falling to the ground in pain for the second time.

'Stop it, stop it!' Jenny was screaming as she came running across the lot.

The hunter barely glanced at her. 'Butt out, girly! This ain't none of your business. I don't give a shit if he is your boyfriend. I want my buck back. Now.'

'He's a foreigner. He doesn't understand. He doesn't speak English. I told you that.'

While Jenny occupied the hunter's attention, the starman had regained his wind as well as his footing. Now he approached and tapped the hunter on the shoulder.

'Excuse me.'

'What?' The hunter turned. As he did so, the starman executed a perfect left-hand feint in imitation of the hunter's earlier fake. The hunter went with it and caught a right cross that sent him skidding on his tail end across the pavement.

'Bingo.' The starman inspected his fist with evident satisfaction.

The stand-off was short-lived. The downed hunter's buddies had been content up till now merely to watch. With their friend hurt they came piling out of the cafe and into the starman. Their target fought back valiantly, but with a repertoire consisting of a single feint and punch, soon found himself on the losing end of the fight.

It was about to get serious when three sharp, echoing bursts from a forty-five brought the conflict to an abrupt

106

end. The three hunters halted their blows in midpunch to stare back at the Mustang. Jenny stood there, pointing the pistol skyward. She nodded toward the hunter the starman had flattened. The man was still wondering what had hit him.

'Pick up your garbage and get going!' Jenny told them.

Another figure came out of the cafe, detaching herself from the crowd that had been drawn by the gunshots. The waitress put a comforting arm around Jenny's shoulders.

'You okay, honey?'

Jenny lowered the muzzle of the gun and the three standing hunters stiffened. They were having a hard time getting their buddy back onto his feet. 'Yeah. Now I am. Thanks for caring.'

The waitress licked her lips, her gaze moving from the hunters to the young woman standing next to her. 'Okay. I just wanted to tell you that the eastbound bus is about to leave. Want me to try and hold it a little longer? I know the driver. He's a regular and he'll do it if I ask him. But he won't be able to wait long.'

Jenny shook her head. The onlookers had vanished, presumably to reboard the bus. 'Never mind. Thanks, but – never mind.'

The waitress nodded, dug into her apron. 'I expect you'll be wanting this stuff back.' She returned the map, keys, and credit card. 'You sure you're okay?'

Jenny smiled reassuringly. 'I'm fine now. Both of us are. Go back to your tables and thanks again.'

'All right. If you're sure.' She turned on her heel and headed back toward the cafe.

Jenny walked over to the starman. He'd recovered his property and turned to face her. 'I thought guns make you little bit jumpy, Jennyhayden.'

'You make me little bit jumpy, remember?' She reached up to touch his battle-scarred face. 'You look like you've been in a war.'

'Define "war."'

'Not now.' She searched through her purse until she found her handkerchief. 'We can't have you walking around like that, bleeding all over everything.' She handed

107

him the bit of cloth, 'Here, wet this.'

He eyed her blankly. She dampened it herself and set about wiping the gore and grime off his forehead. Such a familiar forehead, familiar in every detail. She moved down to clean out his eyes, his lips. It wasn't easy, working over that face. Emotionally, she was as badly banged up as he was physically.

'I thought I told you to steer clear of those bozos,' she said accusingly as she worked on him. 'We've got to get you looking halfway human again.' Suddenly she realized what she'd said and almost broke out laughing.

'I am sorry,' he said contritely. 'I thought . . .'

She touched his lips with the handkerchief, stilling his apology. 'It's okay. I understand. I think.' She searched the pavement until she found the somewhat battered baseball cap, set it firmly back on his head. After a moment's hesitation she turned it around so that the bill was on back to front.

'Looks better that way.'

He nodded and started for the Mustang. 'Thank you, Jennyhayden, for your help and your concern.'

She smiled jauntily. 'All part of our friendly Earth service. We don't do windows, though.'

'I do not understand.'

'Skip it.'

By this time the hunter who'd precipitated all the trouble had recovered sufficiently to watch as his tormentor climbed into the green car across the lot. He tried to follow, but his friends held him back.

'Lemme go! Lemme at the bastard. Goddammit, Donnie-Bob, let me loose!'

Jenny noticed the commotion and hurriedly turned the key in the Mustang's ignition. It was time for them to get out of there. The last thing she wanted was to be anywhere in the bellicose hunter's vision when he fully recovered his senses.

Unfortunately, her nerves were still jangled and she drove for the lot exit a bit too fast. At the same time the hunter broke away from his friends and staggered wildly toward her, stumbling into the path of the oncoming car. As

108

she hit the brakes his friends managed to grab him and yank him out of the way. The Mustang skidded past, fishtailing and stalling out. One of the men tried to get his arms around his irate companion while calling to her.

'Hey, take it easy!'

'I'm sorry,' she shouted back at him, trying to coax the engine back to life. 'I just want out of here!'

Observing this verbal byplay, the starman decided it would be a propitious time for a display of politeness. Recalling his last polite parting he extended the middle finger of his right hand, as he'd seen the trucker at the service station do, and smiled broadly at Donnie-Bob and friends.

'Up yours.'

Already luckless and buckless, the hunter's eyes nearly popped out of his head as he went from furious to near incoherent. 'I'm gonna kill that sumbitch!'

Jenny wrestled frantically with the ignition. 'Oh my God – start. Come on, damn you, start!'

The Mustang growled to life. She burned rubber as she roared blindly out onto the highway, the tires squealing as she fought for control and Donnie-Bob's fingers just scraping the door on the passenger side. His face was livid.

'Come on, dammit!' the hunter yelled. He and his companions piled into the old sedan. The ancient V-8 rumbled and he spun the car backward, threw it into drive, and thundered out onto the highway – straight into the side of the eastbound bus, which was just emerging from the other end of the parking lot.

Heads bounced. The front of the sedan crumpled and steam rushed skyward. Inside the bus, there were curses and a few yelps from startled passengers who had just settled in for the next leg of the long cross-country haul. A six year old began to bawl.

Calm and cool, the driver reassured his charges before climbing down to the ground. He walked slowly toward the sedan. Inside the bus, faces pressed against glass as the passengers followed his progress and anticipated the forth-coming confrontation.

Sheepish faces stared out of the car at him. He crossed

behind it, peered in the driver's window and said danger-ously, 'Well?'

'It was their damn fault!' the driver, whose name was Buzz, informed him. He nodded westward, down the highway. 'The ones in that Mustang. Sumbitch stole my deer and hit me, and when we tried to talk to him, his girl friend pulled a gun on us.'

'Hmmm.' The driver considered this, turned to stare down the road. The scenario this wildman was describing didn't seem very plausible, but then, he hadn't seen anything until the sedan had rammed into his bus. Anyway, it wouldn't be up to him to adjudicate. 'Anybody get his number?'

'They shouldn't be too hard to pick up.' Buzz was feeling better already. 'Seventy-seven green Mustang with Wiscon-sin plates. Can't be too many of those in this part of the country.'

'Nothing personal, bud,' the driver replied quietly, 'but we'll let the cops decide who's at fault here.'

'Yeah, sure. That's fine with me,' said Buzz. 'I just want to meet that guy again, that's all.'

Jenny kept the Mustang cruising along at the regulation fifty-five mph as they cruised down Interstate 80. She didn't want to attract any attention. As soon as it became apparent no one was following them she'd begun talking nonstop, as much to hear her own voice as to say anything.

Besides, the starman was nothing if not a good listener. Just now she was rambling on about her brief married life.

'We met last winter, Scott and I. Up at Iron Mountain. I went to go ice skating. He was up there skiing. He was good, too. See, he did construction work in the summer and taught skiing in the off season. Worked out pretty good for him.

'Anyway, he tried to get me to give it a shot. So I said okay, I'd try skiing if he'd try skating, and he surprised the hell out of me by agreeing. Actually I think it was my outfit that intrigued him, not my Olympic potential. I used to skate competitively. Just small stuff, local contests, but I had one outfit made up, real tight, you know? I don't think he

110

wanted to teach me to ski any more than he wanted to learn how to skate. But he tried hard, and he did okay for a beginner. Skating and skiing are nothing alike. You use different muscles, have to balance completely differently.

'One of the things I liked about him right away was that it didn't bother him to fall down. You get a lot of guys try something like skating and they can't take failing. Scott would land on his can and he'd just grin and laugh it off, then get up and try again. No macho ego problems at all. You don't run into many guys like that, especially good-looking ones.

'One thing led to another and a couple of months later we were on our honeymoon.'

'Honeymoon is nice?'

She glanced sharply at him. He'd been so quiet that she'd almost forgotten he was there. 'Ours was – beautiful.'

'Define "beautiful."'

Her expression turned wistful. 'Beautiful like that is – better than terrific. Better than Dutch apple pie with whipped cream. Beautiful is like what you did to that deer back there in the parking lot. It's the best of everything.'

She was quiet, but this time not for long. Maybe it was his presence, the fact that she had someone to listen to her who wouldn't make moral judgments or offer up false platitudes. Now that she no longer feared him she found there was something calming about being in his presence. She discovered she could replay the fatal accident in her mind without breaking down.

'We went to California and everything was great. But honeymoons are always great. Then we got back and everything was even better and I thought, wow, this is the way it's *supposed* to be.' She looked away from him for a moment. 'See, I never did have much luck with men. I always seemed to go for the good-looking bastards, and I got hurt a lot. And then I met Scott and he seemed too good to be real.

'Anyways, we made plans, had everything worked out. We were going to have a couple of kids and everything. Working two jobs, Scott made good money, and he already had that cabin he'd built himself out on the lake.'

111

She gave him a wan smile.

'Three months later he was dead. Just like that. It was an accident. That's what's been so hard to handle, you know? I mean, you walk into a bank and there's a robbery in progress and you catch a stray bullet, that's one thing. Or you're stuck in a plane crash. But a crummy little "industrial accident?"'

'Scott was a contractor, mostly did painting. He was working on a new apartment building when the damn scaffolding broke. Died right there. He was gone before a doctor could get a look at him. Broke his neck. He was twenty-six goddamn lousy years old.

'And you want to know the part that kills me? We'd had a fight that morning. Our first real fight. I was yelling at him for acting like a dumbbell and he banged out of the house mad. You want to know the crazy part, what we were fighting about? Not us, not how we were going to live together, not even money. No, we were fighting about some damn monkey.'

'Monkey?'

'An animal. Like the deer, only a lot more like us humans. It was on some TV show. The monkey had a plate in its head with wires attached to it so they could study its brainwaves or something. Scott thought it was awful that they should do that.'

'What about you, Jennyhayden? You thought it was all right to do that?'

She hesitated before replying. 'Well, yeah, sort of. The whole idea of the experiment was to save lives.'

'What kinds of lives?'

'Our lives. Human lives.'

'Ah, I see. Because human life is more valuable than monkey life. Or deer life.'

'Well, naturally.'

'Because humans are more intelligent? Superior species?'

'That's right.'

'A question. What if even more intelligent species comes here to this planet. Superior to you. As superior to you as you are to monkey life. Is it all right for them to put a plate and wires in your head? To help save their kind of life?'

She stared at him uncertainly. 'Is that what you're really here for? To put plates in our heads?'

He smiled at her. A gentle, reassuring expression that somehow conveyed something more than a human face was capable of. 'I am here to observe and to study, Jennyhayden. Not to victimize. One can learn without damaging, study without victimizing.'

'I tried to explain to Scott, about the show, that the issues at stake were complex. That it wasn't as simple as he made it out to be.'

'Such issues are never simple.' There was quiet between them for a while. 'I think I would have liked Scott.'

'You said you came here to learn. Are you learning?'

He nodded, staring through the windshield. 'A great deal, and more with each moment that passes. Not as I planned to learn. In some ways this is better. Except for the danger, of course.'

'You've learned something about me. What do you think? Do you see me as . . . as a monkey, or a deer?'

Again the comforting smile, this time without turning to look at her. 'I have learned much about you, Jennyhayden, but if you have to ask such a question it is clear that you have not learned very much about me.'

She opened her mouth, decided better of it, closed it and turned her full attention to her driving. Better maybe to think for a change before opening her big, fat mouth.

She concentrated on the road and so did not see the police cruiser that was hiding behind the billboard and the city limits sign. The two men inside were watching for speeders. The radio set on the dash mumbled officiously. The volume had been turned way down and the dispatcher's words were barely intelligible.

One of the men, whose name was Dusseau, sat up and squinted at the Mustang as it sailed past. 'Hey, that Mustang the state boys want. Wasn't that a green seventy-seven with Wisconsin plates?'

113

His sidekick sat up. 'Yep. What about it?'

Dusseau scrambled to get his feet off the dash. 'Kick 'er in the ass. I think we've got the bastard.'

'No shit?' Officer Tripp jammed the car into gear and sent them bouncing out onto the highway.

'Stay back but keep 'em in sight.' Dusseau's head was alive with visions of promotions and awards. 'We want to make sure we handle this one right. No screw-ups.'

'Check.' Tripp was a man of fewer words. 'Get on the horn and patch us through to somebody who knows what this is all about.'

'Gotcha.'

The big army helicopter looked as out of place in the roadhouse parking lot as a power lifter at a crocheting competition. In addition to the chopper's lights, the parking lot was brightly lit by spots atop the roofs of a couple of Nebraska state police cars.

The cross-country bus had departed long ago, having suffered only a dent in its side. Parked off to one side was the hunter's totalled sedan. Mark Shermin stood next to the helicopter, chatting amiably with the waitress from the cafe.

That was where the state trooper was heading when Buzz reached out to draw him aside.

'Dammit, sergeant, we been here since six-thirty this evening. When can we go?'

'Yeah,' said Donnie-Bob petulantly. 'My Arleen's gonna kill me when I get home.'

The sergeant eyed all three of them with obvious distaste. Under that frankly disapproving gaze the trio milled about uneasily, convinced they'd done nothing wrong but feeling guilty nonetheless.

'You can leave as soon as the Federals say so and not a minute before.'

'But we've already told him everything,' Buzz protested. 'Listen, man, we—' but the sergeant had broken away and resumed his march toward the idling helicopter.

Shermin had just finished thanking the waitress for her

114

help. She was heading back toward the cafe as the sergeant approached. The scientist turned to him.

'Find out anything new, Mister Shermin?' the trooper asked.

Shermin shook his head. "Fraid not. They all tell it pretty much the same. The girl had a half dozen opportunities to get away from him and didn't use any of 'em. Not only that, she helped him get away from those three jerks over there. Then the two of them left together, her driving and holding the gun. That sound like any kind of kidnapping you ever heard of, sergeant?'

The trooper shook his head solemnly. Lemon appeared, framed in the open chopper doorway. 'Mister Shermin! They've spotted one green Mustang, Wisconsin plates, going west on Interstate 80! They're pretty sure it's the right year, too.'

'What are they doing about it?'

'Hanging back and waiting for further instructions.'

Shermin muttered under his breath as he bade the sergeant a hasty farewell and ran for the chopper. 'Don't tell me somebody's finally acting sensibly. I may go into shock.' Then, louder, toward the nose of the craft, 'Let's move it, Lieutenant!'

Someone in the forward compartment nodded and the big copter was lifting off before Shermin was completely inside. A very confused sergeant of the Nebraska state police watched until it had been swallowed up by the night.

Now what the hell, he asked himself, is going on?

Six

Jenny had been blinking and shaking her head, trying to stay awake, for the past hour. Now even the head shakes were failing to clear her vision. Her passenger remarked on it.

'Is something wrong, Jennyhayden?'

'Yeah something's wrong. I'm pooped is what's wrong. Tired. It's time to rest. Remember, I told you about it?'

He nodded. 'I remember. What do we do?'

'The same thing my people do whenever they need something and they're out traveling like this. When you need gas you find a gas station. Food, you find a food station.' She was scanning the highway ahead. 'There's a small town coming up. Should be something out on the freeway exit. We need to find a motel. A sleep station, I guess you'd call it.'

She eased the Mustang down the off-ramp, flanked by several large, well-lit signs. There were several places to chose from but she wasn't in any mood to go bargain hunting. The first motel they came to was big and clean and she turned into the parking lot. It was full of cars and she hoped it wasn't full. Shouldn't be, she thought. Not this time of the week.

Even if she wasn't exhausted it's doubtful she would have noticed the lights of the police cruiser following a hundred yards back.

In addition to the large number of cars there were a couple of big yellow buses parked in the lot. BEAT IOWA banners were draped across the sides. Pasted to the inside of several windows were smaller pieces of cardboard and paper inscribed with less courteous sentiments. Jenny

116

barely noticed the buses as she located an empty parking space and pulled in.

'Gotta have a couple hours sleep,' she declared to no one in particular. 'Just a couple of hours. Okay?'

He nodded, watched as she pushed the forty-five under her seat. They exited the car together, he following close on her heels as she headed for the main building. On the walkway they passed a couple of very large young men wearing red lettermen's sweaters. They were blasting out the Nebraska fight song enthusiastically and off key.

The starman was pleased. 'More singing.'

'Sort of,' she admitted.

Their passage didn't escape notice. One of the football players turned and yelled at them. 'Yeah, Cornhuskers!'

'Yeah, Cornhuskers!' the starman responded, always willing to please.

The second lineman raised a hand, palm facing outward, and declaimed with mock solemnity, 'Pass, friend.'

Jenny pushed open a glass door. 'I think the office must be through here, if that sign outside was right.'

'What is Cornhusker?' her companion inquired curiously. 'Has it to do with food?'

'Depends on what side of the field you're on,' she replied obliquely.

'What side of field food grows on?'

'Never mind. It's getting more complicated than it needs to be and I'm too tired for word games right now.' She sighed. 'Let's just find the front desk, okay?'

Unsatisfied but compliant, he nodded. 'Okay, Jenny-hayden.'

Keeping well away from the green Mustang, the police cruiser crawled into the parking lot. Dusseau kept his eyes on the target vehicle as he addressed the radio mike.

'Looks like they've stopped, maybe going to spend the night here. We could take 'em easy if they've rented a room.'

'No.' The reply from the speaker was firm. 'You are not, repeat *not*, to approach them. Under any circumstances. Just keep them under close surveillance until the Federals

117

get there.'

Tripp made a disgusted sound out of range of the mike's pickup, then leaned over again so he could be heard. 'What if *they* approach *us*?'

There was a pause. They could envision the dispatcher waiting for instructions, listening to someone unseen and unheard.

'If you're in some kind of life-threatening situation, defend yourselves accordingly. But otherwise, wait for the Federals. Out.'

A disappointed Dusseau returned the mike to its holder and found a place to park. Tripp was complaining before the engine died. 'Wait for the Federals, wait for the Federals. They get the six o'clock news and we get the shit end of the stick. We follow these two practically to the damn state line. And for what? A nice pat on the butt when it's all over. Nice doggy cop, good boy. Here's a nice gold star for your record. Well I don't like it. The whole deal sucks.'

'That's the way it is.' Dusseau shrugged. He was watching the green Mustang and the motel beyond, doing his job. Stoic as hell. But he wasn't any happier about their instructions than was his partner.

'Doesn't have to be.' A sly smile slid over Tripp's face.

Dusseau frowned at him. 'What are you talking about?'

The other officer unsnapped the riot gun from its holder, removed it from the rack and checked the chamber. The twelve-gauge pump was full and ready for action, and so was he.

'Maybe nothing, but I got this hunch that this just might develop into a life-threatening situation.'

A blast of sound washed over Jenny and the starman when they entered the coffee-shop annex. Tables and chairs had been shoved aside to create a big open area in the middle of the room. The noise came from a stereo with the bass turned up too far and from the crowd of college students who occupied the makeshift dance floor. Male and female, black and white, all were strenuously doing their best to celebrate their team's forthcoming victory over their interstate rival.

118

Nondancers sat on chairs or cuddled in corners, generating their own private festivities. Spectators stood on table-tops and clapped, urging on the more active celebrants. A bunch of guys clustered around a beer keg while others slaked their thirst from bottles and cans. Several members of the Big Red marching band, uniforms and hats askew, were warming up in a corner and adding the blare of their instruments to the general din.

A girl in a cheerleader's outfit came running past the two newcomers. She was being ardently pursued by a young man clad in white shorts and an open-necked shirt. His tie was fastened around his forehead instead of his neck.

'Wait a minute, Betty! I just want to show you something.'

She yelled back over her shoulder. 'I know, I know. Why do you think I'm running?'

They disappeared outside. The starman followed their progress with interest. He found the sights and sounds surrounding him fascinating.

'Boys will be boys,' Jenny murmured.

'They are going on their honeymoon? If so, why does she run from him?'

'So he'll chase her. This isn't what you think. Honeymoon's later. This is more like your basic primitive mating ritual.'

'Mating ritual?'

'Like boy meets girl.' She eyed him sideways. 'The things I end up explaining to you. Don't you have that either? No sleep, no food, and no that? What do you do with your nights up there, anyway?'

'I do not understand.'

'Never mind.' She turned her attention back to the room, trying to penetrate the swirl of activity surrounding them. 'The sign outside did say that the office was in here. Ah.' She spotted the desk and started toward it, wending her way through swaying beer-drinkers. 'I don't see a clerk. He's probably hiding somewhere in the back.'

Students and the occasional older celebrant made way for her. Sure enough, the clerk popped into view an instant after she rang the desk bell. At the same time the recorded music was turned off in favor of the makeshift dance band and she had to shout in order to make herself intelligible above the renewed roar of the dancers.

'My husband and I – I say, my husband and I would like a room. As far away from this as possible.'

The clerk grinning ruefully. 'I can get you one in Lincoln.'

'Very funny. We'll take the best you can manage. We've been on the road all day and we're both dead tired.'

'You'll have to be, to sleep through this.' He shoved a register full of preprinted forms across the desk. 'King or double?'

'Anything, so long as it's halfway quiet.'

'Ain't got no such animal tonight, but I'll do the best I can. Here.' He handed her a pen. She filled out the registration slip and handed over her credit card, waited as he ran it through the machine, then accepted her receipt and the room key.

'You're down at the end here,' the clerk told her, pointing to a map of the motel layout. 'Second floor. Maybe this bunch'll run down around two or three in the morning, but I doubt it. Good luck.' He turned and vanished into a back room.

She turned. 'Okay, we're all set. Maybe if we turn the air conditioner on high it'll drown out some of this noise. We can—' she broke off, looking around anxiously, suddenly aware she was talking to empty air. 'Hey?'

The starman had disappeared.

'Great,' she muttered. At least he couldn't incite those around him to riot, like he had the hunters. The riot was already in full swing. She started hunting through the crowd for him.

Under the tutelege of and direction from the band, most of the celebrants had formed a line and were snake-dancing their way out into the motel's central courtyard, heading for the big swimming pool. The starman was in the lead, mimicking the steps and swaying perfectly in time to the music. Jenny wasn't surprised to see that he appeared to be having himself a fine old time.

120

Unfortunately, the line was twisting straight toward the pool and she didn't know if he had the vaguest idea how to swim. She rushed toward him.

He stopped by himself, however, breaking away from the head of the line to stare down at the water. The cheerleader and her pursuer were standing in the shallow end, locked in a damp embrace. He stared at them intently. They were much too involved in each other to notice the attention the stranger was devoting to their activities.

So absorbed in study was he that he didn't notice that he was about to be run down by the rest of the snake dancers. Jenny grabbed him and dragged him, still staring at the pool, out of the way. She led him up the stairs toward the second floor of the room complex across the way. He followed unquestioningly, though he kept glancing back over his shoulder toward the water.

Up on the second floor she pointed toward the end of the walkway. 'Go on, go stand over there out of the way and try to stay out of trouble while I check out our room.'

Obediently, he turned and moved to the end of the walkway. Once there he found himself staring at a big blue soda machine which was receiving the angry attentions of one of the Nebraska lettermen. The kid was whacking it repeatedly with one hand. He glanced up at the starman's approach, indicated the machine and explained.

'Damn thing's busted. Ate my sixty cents.'

'Broken?' The starman examined the device.

'Yeah. That's what I said.' He jerked a thumb down toward the central courtyard and the mass of milling students. 'Sometimes a guy wants something besides a beer, y'know?'

Instead of replying, the stranger ran a finger along one side of the dispenser, then passed his palm over the front. Satisfied, he put his hand against a chosen spot and pressed lightly.

Something deep inside the machine went *whang*. This was followed by an echoing, clanking sound, following which Cokes and quarters began erupting from their respective slots. The letterman gaped at the machine, then at the solemn-faced stranger.

'Hey, how'd you do that?' he asked, even as he was dropping to his knees to start grabbing up quarters.

The man gave him a thin but pleasant smile. 'Yeah, Cornhuskers.' Before the letterman could reply a young woman appeared, took in the scene, and started dragging her companion back up the walkway. The astonished football player was too busy clutching at coins and drinks to follow.

'For God's sake,' she snapped at him, 'can't I leave you alone even for a minute without you getting into some kind of trouble?'

'Yeah, Cornhuskers.'

She sighed. 'Right, that makes everything okay. Please try and stay out of trouble. For my sake, okay?'

'I am sorry if I did something wrong, Jennyhayden.'

She glanced back down the walkway. It was deserted except for the letterman, who continued stuffing his pockets unaware that he was the recipient of that evening's dose of interstellar largesse.

'It's okay. Just don't do it again.' She pushed in the door, led him into their room. It was clean, spacious, and more expensive than necessary, but on this trip the last thing she was concerned about was exceeding some imaginary budget.

'Look, I'm going to take a bath. Soak myself in water. As hot as I can stand it.'

'Why?'

'To get clean and to try to relax a little.' She stepped past him, made sure the safety latch on the door was hooked. 'You stay put.' She glanced around the room once more, then crossed to the television and turned it on. 'This knob controls the channels, see?' She demonstrated for him. 'And this is the volume. Think you can watch TV and stay out of trouble while I'm in the tub?'

'I think so, Jennyhayden.'

'Fine.' She headed for the bathroom.

Class place, she decided after closing the door behind her. Free shampoo, shower cap, the works. She turned on both taps, adjusting flow and temperature until they were just as

122

she wanted them. Steam began to rise from the tub.

Better double-check on him, she told herself, just to make sure.

She was worrying needlessly. He was sitting just as she'd left him, in the chair opposite the TV, watching the late night news. She wondered what he thought of it but was too tired to ask him.

'Good,' she murmured, more to herself than to him. 'Oh boy, am I whipped.' She began to undress, kicking off her shoes, pulling off her blouse and then wiggling out of her jeans.

'My mother always told me that there wasn't anything wrong with the world that a hot bath, a good night's sleep, and . . .'

She had her thumbs hooked under the waistband of her panties and had them half shoved down when she stopped. The starman had turned from the set and was staring at her. His expression was unreadable.

'What the hell am I doing?' she mumbled. She scanned the room before crossing to the bed and pulling the spread off. It made a bulky but serviceable sari. 'I'm sorry,' she told him. 'It's just that in this light you're so much like him. I guess I'm getting punchy. I . . .'

'You said the nose is different.'

'What?'

'You said.' He hesitated briefly, then repeated her words. Words she'd all but forgotten. His inflection and pacing were identical to her own, but at least he used his Scott-voice now instead of mimicking hers. 'Your nose is different cause he broke his twice and there's something else, I dunno, something spooky about your eyes.'

'Word for word.' She stared at him in wonder. 'Do you remember everything you hear like that, word for word?'

'Everything I hear. Everything I see. Everything I – this body – feels. It is my job.' Suddenly a splashing sound made her eyes go wide. She turned and charged for the bathroom, the bedspread flapping like a cape around her half-naked form.

'The tub!'

The door slammed behind her. The starman stared after her, listening to the sound of faucets being hurriedly turned. The distant flow of water ceased. He stared at the door for several moments before turning his attention once again to the flow of two-dimensional images appearing on the front of the video device.

Still the news. Sports now, including slow-motion replay of the conclusion of a bloody prizefight. Football scores, then footage of a hotel fire with brave men rescuing children and old people. The weather, with satellite photos of cloud formations scudding across the continental United States. The starman didn't move, his eyes never wavered from the screen. And all the time he spent watching he was analyzing as well as storing.

Because his job involved more than the mere acquisition of information. He would be expected to render opinions as well.

Half an hour later Jenny emerged from the bathroom, wrapped in the bedspread, and promptly collapsed on her side of the bed. She crawled under the covers, discarded her temporary covering, and in minutes was sound asleep.

On the TV the news made way for commercials, then a movie. The starman recognized the film as a simulation, rather than a realistic representation of reality. Frequent commercial interruptions further confirmed his initial deduction.

On the screen, two figures were rolling about on an unknown beach. They were entwined in one another's arms, kissing passionately. Now the starman's attention shifted back to the sleeping Jenny. Back to the scene unspooling on the TV, then back to Jenny again. Television, bed, television, bed.

The scene concluded, made way for a fat man in a funny hat hawking used cars. He was talking a mile a minute from his perch atop an elephant. The starman noted the elephant for future reference. Then he rose and moved over to the bed, sitting down on the side next to the somnolent Jenny. He ran the scene he'd just watched back through his memory, wanting to be sure of the details. Then he bent toward her.

She turned over in her sleep. He crossed to the other side of the bed, sat down again, and lowered his face toward her.

There was a thunderous knocking at the door. He jumped off the bed and stared at it in alarm.

'Hey there, buddy! You in there?' It was a voice he'd heard before. He recognized the speech pattern and tone of the young human whose cents had been eaten by the red machine.

Jenny was sitting up in bed now, blinking sleepily and clutching the sheet to her chest as the starman crossed to the door.

'Wait – no.' She was trying to will herself awake.

'It is all right. I know who it is.' He opened the door. The letterman stood framed in the portal.

'Listen buddy, it's none of my business, but if that's your green Mustang out there in the lot there's a couple of cops trying to jigger the door.'

Tripp worked the wire through the weather stripping, started easing the loop on the far end toward the door latch.

'Hurry it up.' Dusseau was looking nervously toward the motel.

'Why? What's the rush? They've just checked in. They ain't going anywhere except maybe to beddy-bye. Take it easy. Everything's going to work out fine.'

As he finished this there was a loud scraping sound from the vicinity of the motel courtyard which was followed by a tremendous splash.

'What the hell was that?' Dusseau muttered.

'I dunno. Better check it out.' Tripp left the wire dangling through the weather stripping as he followed his partner toward the motel.

The central courtyard was drenched and everything smelled of chlorine. It was Dusseau who spotted the big Coke machine lying on the bottom of the pool, bubbling forlornly. The courtyard was deserted.

From the parking lot came the sound of a big engine turning over. The two men exchanged a glance, then turned as one to race back through the breezeway that led into the motel. They reached the lot just in time to see the green Mustang swing off the pavement and out onto the highway.

'The bastards ran one on us!' Tripp led the rush to their cruiser, threw himself into the driver's seat. Sirens and lights flashing, they peeled out in pursuit.

Peering into the rearview mirror, the starman detected the trailing lights. 'What means?' he asked Jenny.

She turned and looked through the rear window. 'Oh, crap! The police are after us. Authorities.'

He nodded and floored the accelerator.

Dusseau picked up his mike, spoke into it as Tripp tried to keep the taillights of their quarry in sight. 'Papa Charlie Three. Suspects in green Mustang heading south at high speed on US two-eight-one. We are in pursuit intending to overtake.' He shut off the receiver before anyone could think to order them not to.

Utilizing all his newly learned driving skills the starman wove in and out of traffic expertly. Two more patrols cars manifested themselves in the rearview mirror, joining the chase behind Dusseau and Tripp's cruiser.

They were nearing the on-ramp leading to Interstate 80. The starman never slowed, squeezing into the southbound lanes barely in front of an eighteen-wheeler.

Jenny covered her eyes. The starman straightened out, just missing the stern end of another big truck, and stepped on the gas again as the police car accelerated to parallel them.

He reached beneath the seat to bring out the forty-five. Tripp saw it immediately.

'Watch it! He's got a gun.'

As the starman raised it, Jenny looked over and saw what was happening. She knocked his arm down, leaned out her window and screamed, 'No!'

Too late. Tripp had the riot gun aimed and let fly. The blast blew a hole through the passenger side of the Mustang, shattering metal and glass and sending splinters flying through the car. Somehow the starman retained control. The door absorbed most of the force of the shot – but not all. Jenny caught the rest. She slumped against the starman.

Blood was already starting to stain her blouse.

'Jennyhayden!' Her eyelids fluttered as she stared blankly up at him. She made an attempt to speak but nothing came out. Her mouth moved soundlessly. She looked more surprised than hurt.

As the highway split, the Mustang pulled away from the police cruiser. Dusseau was trying to drive while arguing vociferously with his trigger-happy partner. The eastbound lanes became separated from the westbound by a steep rocky island. The glint of a river was visible far below and pine trees began to forest both sides of the road.

The starman fought the wheel as the highway twisted around a stony bluff, tires screaming. They were speeding uphill now. Both pursued and pursuers were forced to slow as their respective engines labored against the sharp gradient.

Far ahead, atop the crest of the hill where the road leveled off, were six stationary vehicles. The starman saw them, glanced again into the rearview mirror. There were now four police cars in the Mustang's tail. He made a quick appraisal of the route ahead. Yes, there ought to be room on the side of the road, there between the pavement and the first big boulders.

The Mustang whipped past the first stopped car, cut into the highway's flank and threw up a huge cloud of dust and gravel. A few of the occupants of the parked vehicles had seen the Mustang coming. One man jumped into its path, waving his arms and trying to stop it before it went over the rise. When it became clear the oncoming Mustang wasn't going to stop for anything, the would-be samaritan dove for safety. The other drivers gaped at it as it rocketed past.

From above came the sound of a descending helicopter.

Looking down and out, Shermin could see the Mustang nearing the crest of the hill. He was cursing hopelessly. He was too far away, too late, and helpless. Then there was no more time left anyway, no more time at all.

When the Mustang reached the top of the grade it was doing a hundred and fifteen. It left the pavement and sailed into the sky, started downward in a slow, graceful curve.

Twenty yards from the crest lay the cause of the lineup of stopped cars. The big gasoline tanker was lying jackknifed across both lanes. Unleaded trickled from a broken valve, running across the highway into a ditch on the far side.

The starman saw it looming ahead of him like a beached whale. As the Mustang descended he reached into a pocket of his windbreaker and grabbed convulsively at one of the gray spheres.

That was all there was time to do before the Mustang smashed into the tanker's side. As the horrified drivers of the parked cars shielded their eyes, a gigantic fireball erupted toward the heavens. The big tanker spasmed. The chassis of the Mustang was thrown skyward, a flaming pinwheel that soared downhill.

Lemon was leaning over Shermin's shoulder, all thoughts of chain of command forgotten, peering out the window of the chopper at the inferno below. 'Jesus,' he muttered softly.

Sirens fading, lights still spinning, the pursuing police cars slowed to a halt among the stopped vehicles. Troopers piled out of their cars and joined the other spectators in gazing in horror down at the roaring blaze. Tripp stumbled forward until the heat forced him to halt. Then he turned away and started throwing up.

The helicopter circled over the wreck for a minute, illuminating it with its big belly light. Then it descended, touching down dangerously near the flaming tanker and the skeleton of the burning Mustang.

Shermin was first out, putting up a hand to shade his eyes from the intense red-orange glow. Even at a distance the heat was daunting. Anything within fifty feet of the blaze would be incinerated in seconds.

Shermin was certain nothing could be brighter than that gasoline fire, but he was wrong. He knew he was wrong when he saw the three beams of laserlike light pierce the smoke and flame. The light grew brighter as he stared at it, heedless of any danger to his eyes. It exploded outward in rainbow brilliance, punching through the inferno and the smoke-filled night. And it came from the still flaming corpse of the Mustang.

As he squinted through his tears at the conflagration the door on the passenger's side of the carbonized car fell off its hinges. Something came out. It wasn't on fire, wasn't even smoking, and that was impossible, impossible. But it was happening, he was seeing it. It looked like Scott Hayden – or whatever it was that had chosen to adopt the guise of Scott Hayden. In its arms it held the unconscious and apparently unburned body of Jenny Hayden, and both of them were coming out of the flames on a broad beam of light.

Shermin knew it was happening because everyone else saw it, too. Up on the hilltop several of the onlookers turned and fled in panic. One of the state troopers fell to his knees and commenced to pray. The rest just stood there in shock and stared, unable to move. The smoke grew dense around them.

Something surrounded Jenny Hayden and the being who cradled her in his arms. Something different from the ashes and flames. It flickered and pulsed, enclosing them in a protective cocoon of polarized light. It was at once beautiful and terrifying.

The starman was staring hard at his surroundings, and this time the expression on his face wasn't a mimickry of something seen before. It flowed straight out of the basic, raw human emotion his human frame was heir too. It was not controlled, and it was full of anger.

The light breeze which had sprung up in the wake of the tanker's explosion now died. Smoke closed in tightly around the impossibility. Police and onlookers alike began coughing and running in search of cleaner air. Shermin stood there, coughing his lungs out, until Lemon came and pulled him bodily back inside the helicopter.

Night closed in and hid what the thick black smoke did not.

Seven

The wreckage was still smouldering the following morning when the big truck wrecker finally succeeded in dragging it off to the side of the road. Firemen stood ready nearby and continued to drench the steaming metal frame, alert lest the heat spread fire to the surrounding brush. Tired police began directing the long line of backed-up traffic around the seared splotch of highway. Exhausted drivers, many of whom had spent the night discussing what they thought they'd seen amidst the smoke and confusion, climbed back into their cars and prepared to resume their interrupted travels.

One cop had been delegated to break the good news to the impatient truckers. 'All right, all clear up ahead. Let's crank 'em up and move 'em out, boys!'

'With pleasure!' replied the first in line. His colleagues readily agreed with him, though they voiced their feelings in more colorful terms as they scattered to their respective rigs.

The growls of big Detroit diesels filled the crisp dawn air, sending foraging birds racing for quieter climes. One at a time the big trucks moved out into the newly opened lanes.

One extra-long flatbed had half a mobile home lashed to it. As he headed for his cab, the driver noticed that one of the bottom flaps of the polyethelene sheet that sealed off the center of the home-to-be had become unfastened. He pulled the loose tab through an eyebolt and tied it securely before climbing into his cab and firing up the engine.

The starman lay motionless on the floor of the mobile

home, waiting and listening as the truck started to move. Despite his best attempts to cushion Jenny, the sudden jostling woke her. She cried out in pain and looked up at him without seeing him. Then her eyes glazed over again. Her breathing had become slow and labored. Her right side was covered with dried blood where the blouse had been soaked through.

The bouncing eased once the big truck was back out on the smooth highway and up to speed. Their driver knew his business and ran through the gears with nary a jerk.

Moving on his belly, the starman crawled to the edge of the half house and lifted the lower edge of the plastic seal. Scenery was racing past. The air was warm and dry. There were no signs of following police. He let the flap fall back into place and hurried back to Jenny.

She had lapsed into unconsciousness. After a moment he removed her blouse and compared his skin color to her own. He knew that pigmentation varied widely among humans, but Jenny's was too pale even for her own light-skinned type. Gingerly, he moved her right arm away from her body so he could check her side. She was still bleeding. She wouldn't last through the day.

He put a hand over her heart, moved it slowly up to her forehead. He could hear the air flowing slowly in and out of her chest. Comparing his own body to hers, he discovered that her heartbeat had become slow and irregular. The life-support system that was the human body was less complex than many he had studied. Jenny's was hovering dangerously close to failure.

He reached into a pocket and brought out the two remaining gray spheres. One he slipped back into the windbreaker. The other he crushed in his right hand. Light and heat began to emerge from between his clenched fingers.

He started with her face, where a piece of shattered window glass had cut the skin. The resultant wound was jagged and ugly. Placing the hand holding the sphere over the site of the injury, he pressed gently. A sharp pain went

131

through him but he did not move his hand. The sphere would not do such work by itself. There had to be organic input from an outside source, and he was the only source available. It put considerable strain on his already weakened self, but there was no thought of hesitating.

When he finally pulled away his hand he was relieved to see that the wound had disappeared without leaving a scar. He'd been especially careful about that. Repeated observations indicated that these people placed great store in their facial appearance.

More confident now, he went to work on her side and the darker, deeper injuries there. Her skin became almost transparent. Deep within her body, small fragments of lead shot began to glow as the starman manipulated the healing energies of the sphere. He was struggling both to seal the wounds the shotgun had produced and to reduce the imbedded metal to harmless particles of microscopic size. He worked slowly and with patience. It was not the first time, after all, that he had worked on a human body. He'd already fashioned one for himself.

It took time. The body would make use of the iron, but the lead would have to be completely eliminated from Jenny's system. It was a complicated piece of work.

Once, the whole rig swerved violently as the driver was forced to cut in front of a couple of old pickups doing no better than forty. The starman gritted his teeth and held his position, not daring to break the healing chain that linked him to Jenny. If it was broken now, there might not be enough energy left in the sphere to reestablish the bridge.

Eventually the time came when the last of the damaging pellets had been dissolved, the final nerves and blood vessels repaired. Letting out a long sigh of relief and exhaustion, he sat back against a kitchen cabinet and cradled her in his arms. It was easy to check her vitals and he was gratified to observe that both her breathing and heartbeat had returned to normal.

'It was my fault.' Even as he whispered to her he was

132

aware of the absurdity of the apologia. She was sound asleep and couldn't hear a word he said, but for some reason voicing the *mea culpa* aloud in the alien tongue made him feel better. 'My fault. I am so sorry.'

As he sat there, listening to the miles slide past beneath the flatbed's thick tires, he thought back to something he'd learned not long ago while watching the visual communications device. It was something he'd been wanting to try. Under the present circumstances it took on a new significance.

He bent over and kissed her lightly. She did not respond, though she stirred ever so slightly in her sleep. His human form did. It was the simplest and most uncomplicated gesture he had performed since he'd assumed his human shape.

It was also in many ways the most enlightening.

The bird woke Jenny. Cars and trucks had been coming and going all around her for hours and she'd slept through everything. But there's something about the raucous call of a blue jay that's just as penetrating if not quite as loud as an air horn. It made her blink.

She was lying on the floor of a house, only it was a funny kind of house. There was no furniture, only built-ins. Linoleum was smooth and cool beneath her. Raising her head enabled her to see a sink and dishwasher, cabinets and countertops, but not a hint of decoration.

There was also something that didn't belong in any house: the sound of a CB blasting away somewhere nearby.

'Flash for all you good buddies heading west on seventy,' the heavily accented voice was declaiming. 'They've got a roadblock in place just out of Grand Junction. Don't ask me why, but better dump your dope and anything else you oughtn't to have. Looks like this is serious business. They're takin' names and kickin' ass.'

A crackling sound as other voices all tried to join in simultaneously. Jenny was fully awake now. What had happened? She'd been asleep, and soundly for the first time in days. She felt refreshed and fully rested. That didn't make any sense. It didn't make any sense because . . .

She remembered the shock of the impact as the slugs from the riot gun had torn into her side, remembered the dizzying pain before the darkness had engulfed her. She sat up and the windbreaker that had been covering her fell off. Dazed, she looked down at it. It was his.

Her eyes went to her ribs, her hands to her face. The skin was smooth and unmarred. But – she'd been shot. She remembered it clearly, remembered the feel of the window glass tearing into her cheek as she'd tried to turn away. The gun had been so close, had hurt so bad. As a little girl she'd been kicked in the side by a horse. That was what the shot reminded her of. But there was no evidence of it now, except for the memory.

There was something else, too. On her right side beneath the last rib she'd had a mole, ever since she could remember. Not a big one, but she'd always worried about it despite numerous doctors' repeated insistence that it presented no danger to her. It was gone too.

What had happened? Had everything been a dream?

Another piece of clothing lay nearby. She reached over and picked up the blouse she'd been wearing, unfolded it and saw the extensive bloodstains. Her blood. It covered half the blouse, the entire right side and all the way around at the waist. End of dream theory.

Slipping into the windbreaker, she zipped up the front and began searching the floor. Her purse lay nearby. She ignored it, stood up and started through the other rooms. The CB outside came to life again.

'The block's on I-70 just east of Grand Junction. It's not just local smokies, either. There's army paratroopers out there too and they're checking papers. Any you illegal beagles out there drivin' better detour down through Delta. Way I hear it is they're lookin' for some young stud who's supposed to have kidnapped a chick . . .'

Jenny's eyes went wide. Grand Junction? That didn't sound like Nebraska. Colorado, maybe. How long had she been unconscious? It was morning outside. Only one night, then. Somehow her wounds had healed completely over-night. Look as she might, she couldn't find a single scar, much less any sign that she'd taken a shotgun blast in the ribs. There wasn't much doubt about the source of her miraculous cure. The resurrected deer was still fresh in her memory.

But where was he?

She crossed to the side of the house and slipped under the bottom edge of the thick polyethelene sheet, found herself standing in an expansive parking lot. There were a half dozen eighteen-wheelers parked neatly side by side like ships in a Navy yard, a few cars, several RVs, and one beat-up but flashy pickup equipped with chrome roll bar, a big number thirteen painted on its hood and doors, and enough spotlights to illuminate the big room at Carlsbad Caverns.

At the back of the parking lot was a long, low single-story building that looked as old as the surrounding mountains. The sign above the entrance read ELMO'S. She hurried toward it.

The booths and the counter were busy. A small horde of tourists and quietly chatting truckers were deep into breakfast. She didn't give a thought for subtlety and had no time for it anyway.

'Who's hauling the mobile home?' She had to shout to make herself heard over the peripatetic children. Few of the tourists bothered to look up, but all the truckers did.

One of them replied. 'I am. Why?'

She walked over to him. His companions silently bemoaned their lack of potential good fortune and returned to their meals.

'I'm looking for a fella,' she said softly. 'He might've been riding on the back of your rig. About twenty-six. Brown hair, eyes, six foot, one seventy or so. Chinos, red plaid shirt. Might've passed him on the road hitchhiking if he wasn't with you.' She raised her voice, repeated the description and the query. 'Anybody? Anybody see him?'

A series of denials, followed by a few offers to replace the services of the missing gentleman. She smiled but ignored the latter as she headed for the rear of the restaurant. It was near a back door and the phone was enclosed.

She shut the double doors behind her and took out her wallet, hunted through it until she found a quarter. Setting the wallet and her purse down next to the phone, she dropped the quarter into the slot and dialed O.

'I want the police,' she told the operator.

Shermin was standing close to the chopper, watching as the paratroopers politely questioned irate motorists and searched car trunks, vans, and campers. The troops weren't his idea. He thought they were too visible. But Fox had insisted. Considering the mess the local cops had made of things Shermin wasn't very vocal in his objections, even though both men knew it was going to make it tougher than ever to keep everything out of the papers. They'd already had to deal with a local UPI stringer out of Denver who'd come sniffing around earlier this morning. Fox had managed to get rid of him by promising him an exclusive later on when the 'real' story broke. The reporter had departed only partly mollified. Shermin knew that the first thing the man was going to do when he got back to Denver was report the whole business to his bureau chief. Then the fat would really be in the fire.

For the moment, though, they had preserved Operation Visitor's anonymity. It wouldn't last forever and they weren't making much progress. They *had* to find him soon, before the media hordes latched onto what was really going on. Then science would lose out to the inevitable circus that would follow. Knowledge of that reality was the main thing that kept two such disparate personalities as Fox and Shermin working smoothly together.

He thought back to the incredible events of the previous night, remembered trying to explain them to Fox.

'Never mind,' the chief of security had finally told him. 'The main thing is that we can't risk a reoccurrence. Next time some innocent bystanders are liable to get blown away. If that happens it'll be my neck as well as yours.'

'Why me?' Shermin had replied. 'I'm just a lousy consultant. Tactics aren't my department.'

136

'Try telling that to a congressional panel of inquiry.'
With that, Fox had broken the connection.

Shermin wished that a congressional panel of inquiry could have witnessed the unexplainable on the highway last night, but he wasn't having much luck lately getting his wishes fulfilled. A voice interrupted his musing. Lemon stuck his head out the chopper door.

'Hey, Mark! You're wanted on the horn. Urgent.'

'Isn't it always,' he muttered as he turned to enter the helicopter. Lemon thrust mike and earphones at him. He slipped the phones indifferently over his head. Probably some local cop who thought he might maybe perhaps possibly have seen their quarry. Every law enforcement officer in the central United States was trying to make a name for himself by finding the fugitive the government wanted so badly. Shermin had resigned himself to dealing with hundreds of false sightings. They couldn't afford to ignore any of them, though. The least positive might turn out to be the most accurate.

Anyhow, talking on the radiophone was more interesting than standing and staring at the roadblock.

Jenny considered hanging up and trying again. 'Hello. Hello? I've been cut off. I was talking to the police, please.'

What had happened to her connection? One minute she'd been talking with a desk sergeant, then with his superior, and the next thing she knew the line was full of beeps and squawks. She was about to hang up when a new voice came on the line. It was pleasant and chatty, reassuringly friendly even over the static.

'Hello, Mrs Hayden? I'm not the police. They very kindly referred your call through to me. My name's Shermin, Mark Shermin. I'm with the National Security Agency.'

She frowned. 'Like the FBI?'

'Sort of. We're just not quite as visible. I understand you wanted to speak with somebody about a kidnapping?'

'Yes. Well, the thing is, there wasn't any kidnapping.'

A pause at the other end of the line. 'I see. You know, I

137

had the opportunity to talk to that real-estate lady of yours, Mrs Hayden – what's her name again? She seemed to think you'd met with some kind of foul play.'

'It's Gretchen Gilman. She's with Gilman Realtors in Ashland. But you probably know that already, since you say you've talked to her. Is she okay?'

'Worried about you is all. There was that bullet hole in the window of your living room. We're all worried about you, Mrs Hayden.'

'Well you don't have to be. I'm fine. I don't know about any bullet hole in my window but there aren't any in me.' Not since he fixed me up, anyway, she reminded herself. 'All I'm calling for is to clear up this business about kidnapping. See, it's kind of complicated, but what's really happening is that . . .'

'Where are you calling from, Mrs Hayden?'

'I don't know. Some truck stop.'

'It's awkward trying to talk like this. Listen, why don't I come and pick you up so we can chat in person? There are so many questions I badly want to ask you.'

Through the doors of the phone booth she could see one of the waitresses coming down the aisle between the booths and the counter. Instead of stopping at a table to take an order, the woman came right up to the booth and rapped on the glass. She was smiling encouragingly.

'Hang on a minute, Mr Shermin.' Jenny put one hand over the receiver and cracked the doors with the other.

'Is something wrong? Does somebody else want to use the phone? I'll just be another minute.'

'Nope.' The waitress jerked her head toward the windows that overlooked the parking lot. 'I heard you talking to the boys. You looking for a guy?' She raised her hand over her head, palm facing downward and parallel to the floor. 'About yea tall? Red plaid shirt? Kind of nice looking?'

Shermin's voice sounded anxious. 'Hello? Mrs Hayden, are you still there?' Jenny ignored him.

'Yes, yes! Have you seen him?'

138

'Sure have.' The older woman turned and gestured toward the highway. 'He hitched a ride west with the night cook about half an hour ago. I saw 'em go out together.'

'Thank you. Thank you so much.'

'My pleasure, honey.' The waitress turned and headed back toward the kitchen.

Jenny spoke rapidly into the phone. 'Listen, mister, I'm hanging up now. I've got to go. If you want to ask me questions, call me in a couple of days at my parents' home in Madison. They're in the book.'

'Wait! Do you know what you were kidnapped by?'

'I told you, I wasn't kidnapped.' She was about to place the receiver on its hook, hesitated, drew it back to her lips a last time. 'Look, he doesn't want to hurt anybody. Really. What happened last night was all the police's fault. He's a little uncertain what to do sometimes, but he only means well. Can't everybody just leave him alone?'

She hung up before Shermin could reply and dashed out of the booth, grabbing her purse as she fled. The phone couldn't hurt her. It was only a phone. But she didn't want to be there if it rang back.

She halted near the doorway, turned to eye the counter and the booths, took a deep breath and said loudly, 'I need a fast ride west!'

Before any of the truckers could respond, a young man clad in flannel shirt and coveralls with the words BARNEY'S BODY SHOP stenciled across the back was halfway to her. 'Let's go!'

She eyed him up and down, decided he was too enthusiastic to be dangerous, and nodded, ignoring the envious mutterings of the truckers. Somewhat to her surprise, he held the door open for her as they left.

Meanwhile Mark Shermin was trying to will the excited, anxious voice back onto the line. 'Hello, hello?' Static buzzed teasingly back at him. He finally handed the receiver back to Lemon. 'Damn it,' he said quietly. 'Did they make the trace?'

The radioman listened a moment, shook his head. 'No

139

luck. They didn't have much time. You were supposed to keep her on the line.'

'I tried dammit.'

'They're still working on it,' the radioman told him, 'but it's—' he broke off as a new voice sounded over one of the auxiliary speakers.

'Project Visitor, this is Comcent calling.'

'Fox again,' Shermin muttered. 'Let's hear what he's got to say this time.'

'You want a private channel?'

'No. Go ahead and pipe it through.'

Lemon nodded, flipped a switch. Shermin was on speakerphone now and could talk to his boss without having to bother with the handheld receiver.

'Yes, sir, I'm here.'

'Shermin? Good. Listen carefully. There are no more ambiguities. I've just left the White House. The orders were clear. We want that alien. We want him alive if possible, but we want him. There's to be no more hide-and-seek playing, even if the media's brought in. We don't know what our visitor's intentions are and some of the military people back here are starting to get real nervous.'

'Meaning what?'

'Meaning that since he hasn't walked into a police station or even a post office to give himself up, the feeling here is that he doesn't intend to do so. So we're going to give him a lift to someplace nice and quiet before he can cause a panic, like he nearly did on the Interstate the other night, and before somebody gets hurt.'

'I've hushed that up, sir. We've no press problems on that one.'

'Fifty people watch a car plow into a gas tanker, blow up, and then the occupants of the car come floating out on a beam of light and you say you managed to "hush it up"?'

'We told the onlookers that we were making a movie.'

'Oh. And they bought it?'

'Why not? It sure as hell looked like something out of a movie.'

140

'Okay, good work, but there's no guarantee we'll be that lucky if something like that happens again.'

'Listen sir, if you want my opinion, I think we ought to . . .'

'I'll be on a plane in fifteen minutes, Shermin. No more pussyfooting around, understand? We want him in custody in twenty-four hours.' The line went dead.

Lemon was sympathetic. 'Tough trying to talk to the top brass, huh?'

'It is when their heads are made of it. Brass, that is.'

'What now?'

Shermin looked back out toward the highway, the long line of vehicles, the sweating troops checking faces and IDs. 'Maybe we get lucky.'

The sign said GRAND JUNCTION – 5 MILES. The old Chevy banged past, its engine and tranmission, not to mention the chassis, held together by love and baling wire. The night cook from Elmo's was no mechanic and he was saving his money for better things. But the car still ran, and the sole passenger did not mind the smell of oil. It was something else to analyze.

The cook was no motor-mouth, but his radio wasn't working and the total silence was beginning to grate. Since his passenger wasn't about to volunteer anything, it behoved him to try to start a conversation.

'What's your line, friend?'

The young man seated next to him seemed to pull his attention back from somewhere far away. ' "Line"?'

'Work. Job, profession, occupation. What do you do when you're not hitchin' rides?'

'Oh.' He considered, decided that a simple answer would be best for a simple question, even if it was a gross oversimplification. 'I make maps.'

The cook perked up. 'Hey, that sounds interesting. I have enough trouble reading the damn things without imagining what it would be like trying to make one.' He nodded at the surrounding mountains. 'Bet you're into oil.

141

There's a lot of oil around here, or so they say. Me, I never seen any of it. Except the kind that comes out of a bottle that I use on my grill.' He grinned. The starman politely grinned back at him.

'You like it?'

'Yes. It is – fulfilling work.'

'Make any money?'

'No. There are other – compensations.'

'Yeah, I can dig that. You don't get rich cookin', either, believe me. But everybody has to do what they can, right?'

'Right.'

'I like the hours. I don't sleep as much as I used to and workin' nights I can be home with the family most of the day. But the money makes it tough sometimes.' A touch of pride crept into his voice. 'I got a girl goin' to college this fall. The wife had to go back to nursing to help pay for it, but we'll manage. Suzy's goin' to have her chance no matter what. First one in the family to go to college. Ain't that somethin'?' He slipped a pack of cigarettes out of his shirt pocket, used his lips to remove one and offered the pack to his companion.

'Smoke?'

The starman accepted the cigarette and watched carefully as the cook adjusted his own in his mouth. He echoed the gesture, fully expecting the man to begin chewing on the thin, aromatic cylinder. Instead, to his considerable surprise, the cook produced a portable source of flame and set fire to the combustible plant material the paper roll contained.

'She wants to be a doctor,' the cook was telling him. 'Like I said, the wife and I are going to do our best, but it worries me. Medical school and all that. 'Course after Suzy gets her degree, she'll be able to work part-time and help out with tuition and stuff. Costs an arm and a leg to raise a kid these days.'

'"Arm and a leg"?' Although unfamiliar with it, the starman immediately perceived this as an idiomatic

142

expression, as the cook still had his full complement of limbs.

'Geetus. Bread. Money, and lots of it.' He reached over to light his passenger's cigarette, then inhaled on his own. The starman managed a passable imitation of the procedure until he began to choke. His eyes reddened and the cook cleared his lungs with a sharp whack on the back.

'Got to watch it. Those Camels can get to you if you're used to the lighter stuff. Me, I got no use for menthol and lights and all that crap. Smokin' all those chemicals is bad for your health. Right?'

'Right.' The starman coughed.

The hopped-up sedan was tooling down the Interstate at nearly eighty miles per hour. Every so often the young driver would take a glance at the radar detector clipped to his sun visor. Each time he checked it it was blank and he'd push their speed up another notch.

'How'm I doing?' he asked his passenger, yelling above the rumble of the engine.

'Fine,' Jenny told him. Then her eyes went wide.

The young man smoothly slid around the big truck ahead of them and cut back just in front of the other truck that had been coming toward them. Jenny hung on for dear life, didn't relax much as they swung back into the safety of the right-hand lane. Behind them, the twin blast of different air horns was already fading.

'Of course,' she added as she fought to get her breath back, 'I'd like to get where I'm going in one piece.'

'Hey, no sweat, sugar. Relax and leave the driving to Dave.' Despite their speed he looked relaxed and confident. Jenny wished she could relax. She thought longingly back to the brief moments of real sleep she'd enjoyed at the big motel.

'None of my business,' he said casually, 'but what did you do?'

'Do?' She eyed him blankly.

He grinned, kept his eyes on the road ahead. 'C'mon, sugar, you don't need to play coy with me. Somebody's

143

after you and I'll bet it ain't your Uncle George.'

'Okay, I'll level with you.' She paused a moment to think up something plausible. 'We robbed a bank.'

'Out-*standing*!' He seemed to straighten a little in his seat. 'How much did you get away with? Where'd you do it? How many are there in your gang? Was there any shooting?'

Terrific, she thought. A TV addict. Well, what the hell. He was taking her where she wanted to go. The least she could do was supply the entertainment. She launched into a lengthy and highly fanciful description of the nonexistent robbery, utilizing every cliché from every cops-and-robbers film she'd ever seen.

Her driver ate it up . . .

The battered old Chevy topped an overpass and pulled off on the ramp. Ahead lay the outskirts of the town of Grand Junction – and something else.

The cook frowned as he studied the highway ahead. One at a time, a seemingly endless line of westbound vehicles was inching its way through a line of army vehicles. Trucks mostly, but a couple of tanks sat off to one side of the main road, their operators conversing lazily. Once in a while an irate traveler would lean on his horn, but for the most part everyone bore the unexpected delay stoically.

'What's the deal? War games of some kind, I guess. We get those guys in from the base all the time. Didn't hear anything about this on the news, though.' He shrugged. 'Boys will be boys. Me, I'm glad I'm too old for that kind of kid stuff.'

The starman turned to him. 'War games?'

'Yeah. Silly, ain't it?' He nodded forward. 'Just the upkeep on one of those tanks would pay my girl's way through medical school. Then we'd have one more doctor in the country to help people. But who am I to say where my tax money's supposed to go? I'm just a citizen, right?' He jerked a thumb toward the side road that climbed away from the Interstate and back into the hills.

'This here's my turnoff. I live right up the road but our

144

trailer's back on a creek. Can't hear the traffic and it's nice and convenient. Don't care much for living in town. Buy you a cup of coffee? The wife's always glad of company.'

'No. I must go.' He reached for the door handle.

'You don't come from around here, do you? This country, I mean.'

The starman hesitated. 'No.'

'You German? Scandinavian, maybe? My grandfather on my mother's side was a Swede.'

'No. Farther than that.'

'I guessed as much. What do you think of it?'

'Think of it?'

'This country. The folks hereabouts.'

He considered the question carefully before replying. 'I don't know yet.'

'But you're workin' on an opinion?'

'Yes.' He pushed down on the door handle and opened the door to let himself out. 'I am working on an opinion.'

There was a lot of dust and an equal amount of confusion as the soldiers tried to keep order among the drivers of the double line of vehicles. Tempers grew shorter as the temperature rose and while most of the drivers handled it well, there were a few who had deadlines to meet and they let the soldiers know what they thought of the holdup in less than polite terms. There was a lot of talk about writing congressmen and the local papers.

For their part, the troops weren't happy about being called away from their comfortable barracks, hustled into trucks, and hauled out into the middle of nowhere to play traffic cop.

It was bad enough having to check every damn trunk, but orders were to search trailers and motor homes as well, to the intense displeasure of the vehicle's owners. There'd already been one casualty: a corporal who'd jerked open the door of a Winnebago before consulting its irate owner, only to find himself face to face with an angry and very territorial German shepherd.

Someone in the middle of the line had decided to amuse

himself by tooting out children's songs on his car horn. Further back in the line a group of younger and less uptight travelers had tuned up their guitars and initiated an impromptu songfest. Neighboring drivers joined in with voices and appreciative handclapping.

Patiently the soldiers carried out their assignments, hoping it wouldn't be much longer until the two people in the photographs they'd been handed put in an appearance.

The cook gave his passenger a farewell half-salute. The starman returned the gesture in kind, watched as the Chevy worked its way up the side road. Then he turned and started walking down the shoulder toward the distant line of vehicles.

Shermin had strolled over to the roadblock. Surveying the travelers waiting to get through, he noted the presence of backpackers and day hikers roaming around and decided he'd better comment on it.

'Better get these pedestrians in line. Some of them are slipping around the end and ignoring the checkpoint.'

'Yes sir.' The lieutenant looked meaningfully at his first sergeant, a career man who wanted nothing more than to be back in the NCO club on the base and instead found himself stuck out here on the highway in the middle of a hot afternoon. 'You heard the man.'

'Right, sir.' Grumbling under his breath the older man turned and began passing the word to his men. 'All right, let's shape it up here!' He called over a couple of hikers, envying them their cool shorts and short-sleeved shirts. 'You folks have to go through the checkpoint just like everybody else. Come on now, I'm not enjoying this any more than you are – pay attention, soldier, and keep 'em in line, will you? All you pedestrians there, line up on the right.' He gave one man who might have been partly deaf a gentle push back toward the processional.

Near the rear of the line the starman obediently took his place. Up ahead, the lieutenant and the sergeant were working their way toward him, checking faces and papers as they came.

146

Eight

The young man slowed. Heat rose in ripples from the hood of his car. 'I guess we missed him. Some kind of roadblock up ahead. I'd better stop here – my rear tires aren't standard and the cops can make trouble for you when they're feeling antsy. I'm sorry.'

'It's not your fault. You did your – oh!' She was staring at the line of people on foot. 'Oh no.'

'What, where?' asked her champion, peering over the wheel and trying to see what had upset her.

She gestured with a wavering finger. 'That's him up ahead, in that line! They'll find him.'

'Like hell they will,' said the young man huskily. He thromped the accelerator and the oversized engine roared.

By this time the starman had grasped the purpose behind the roadblock. The attitudes displayed by the disgruntled drivers nearby and by the people in front of and behind him indicated it was not a normal, everyday occurrence. It had been set up for a special reason.

He saw that the men in uniform who were working their way down the line toward him were carefully inspecting each person before allowing them to continue on their way. He knew that he had to get out of the line before they reached him, but he was surrounded on all sides by armed humans. If he suddenly left and began to run they'd capture him for sure.

A noise made him turn. Something loud and mechanical was coming toward the line at high speed. Everyone turned to look. Some broke and ran as the car came

147

barreling down the shoulder of the Interstate straight toward them.

It executed a sharp U-turn and kicked up a huge cloud of dust, fishtailing through the dirt and weeds. The lieutenant gaped at it like everyone else, then turned to yell an order. As he inhaled, his mouth filled with dust.

In the middle of the brown cloud a door opened. Hands reached out and pulled the gasping, choking starman into the front seat. He wiped his eyes, blinked.

'Jennyhayden!'

'Let's move it, Dave!'

'Roger, wilco, Commander!' Grinning at both of them the young man gunned the engine. The car tore around the outside of the road-block at high speed, kicking up a huge roostertail of dust in its wake. Behind it there was a lot of dirt, cursing, and confusion as the troops tried to get organized. In the swirling dust no one could locate Mark Shermin.

'My God,' Jenny muttered, staring at the starman as the car pulled back onto the concrete with a loud screech, 'what are you doing here?'

'I hitched a ride. With a cook.'

She shook her head. 'Ask a silly question.'

'It is good to see you.'

'You too.' She turned to speak to the driver. 'This isn't going to work, Dave. They'll be on top of us any minute now.'

'No way. You should've seen 'em when we pulled out. They're all running around bumping into each other. Besides, you think I can't outrun a lousy jeep?' He accelerated, staring over the wheel like a man possessed.

'What if they send a couple of helicopters after us?'

'Oh.' He looked crestfallen. 'I didn't think of that.' He slowed, looked over at her. 'What do you want to do?'

'I don't know. Give me a minute to think.' After a pause she nodded toward the side of the road. 'Pull over and let us out.'

He sighed. 'You're the boss, lady.'

The car rumbled to a stop and Jenny and the starman got out. She leaned back in and flashed her sexiest smile. 'Thanks for everything, Dave. You really helped us out of a tight spot.'

'My pleasure. You sure I can't take you any farther?'

'No. We've got to try something else. You go on ahead. Maybe they'll follow you. I don't want you to get into trouble, so if they catch you tell them we forced you to drive us.'

'Gotcha.' She stepped back and watched as the car peeled out, leaving rubber on the concrete. Taking the starman's hand Jenny led him across the highway toward the eastbound lane. Now it was the wind and not a car that was kicking up dust.

A station wagon came toward them, swerved around at the last instant. The driver leaned on his horn and shouted back at them. 'Rent a room!'

'Asshole!'

Jenny gaped at the starman. 'Where'd you learn that?'

'The cook.'

'Great education you're getting.' She stared down the deserted highway. 'We gotta get out of here.'

An old pickup came chuffing along. Jenny stepped out and waved. It slowed down, pulled over next to them. She leaned toward the open window on the passenger side and spoke hopefully. A couple of kids, brown as coffee beans, stared back at her out of wide dark eyes.

'Please, mister, we need a lift real bad. Which way you going?'

The driver was thin, muscular, and almost as dark as the children. His slim mustache was damp with sweat. 'Durango, señora.'

'That'd be swell.'

He jerked a thumb over his shoulder. 'You can ride in the back, if you don't mind some company.'

She smiled up at him. 'Thanks.' They went around to the rear of the truck and she helped the starman climb over the tailgate. As they pulled back out onto the road she took stock of their fellow passengers. There was a young woman with a baby in her arms and an old man. She tried not to stare. There weren't a lot of Hispanics in rural Wisconsin.

'We are going the right way?' the starman asked her.

She nodded, leaned back against the wheel well. 'The guy who got us past the roadblock told me there's a railroad down here that runs almost due south, straight through Winslow. If we can hop a freight it'll take us right into town. From there we can hitch to where you have to go.'

The starman was staring at her intently. Not that he had become an expert on the full range of human emotions as conveyed by vocal inflection, but he was certain her tone was different than he remembered it. Short and strident.

'You sound different. I have done something wrong?'

'Oh no, nothing at all. What makes you think that?' she said sourly. 'I wake up alone inside half a trailer in the middle of nowhere and you're gone. Disappeared, took off, without leaving a note or anything. I thought we were friends.'

'You are right. We are friends. I did it to help you. To be with me is not good for your health. I do not want to see you hurt, Jennyhayden, and because of me you might have died.'

'Friends don't run out on each other like that, no matter what the reason. At least you could've said good-bye.'

'"Good-bye?"'

'You don't say good-bye up there?'

'Teach me this.'

'What's to teach?' She shrugged. 'Good-bye is farewell. It's – hell, I don't know. It's a custom, a politeness. If you say it a certain way it means that, well, it's a way of telling somebody you like that you – wish them well. That you hope . . .'

A loud squalling interrupted her as the baby in the young woman's arms woke up. The mother also came to life, tried to quiet the infant while looking apologetically over at the starman and Jenny.

'Her tooth comin' in. You know.' She gestured to her own mouth. '*Diente*.' She rocked the baby in her arms. '*Pobrecita*. The long ride is hard on her.'

'Can I hold her for a while? You could get some rest.'

'No. *Gracias*, but it is okay. There is nothing anyone can do. We have no medicine.' She smiled bravely. 'I do not like to see her cry, but it will stop soon. The hurt will go away.' As she finished the infant let out another unhappy wail.

Smiling reassuringly at the mother, the starman leaned forward. 'Excuse me, please.'

'You doctor?' She eyed him disbelievingly.

'No, but I can help.' The young woman looked at Jenny, who nodded.

He put gentle fingers on the baby's face, ran them across the cheeks and over the chin, barely skimming the lips. The crying turned into a gurgling sound, gave way to silence as the baby stared up at him out of wide, guileless eyes.

The old man said something for the first time. It was in Spanish and Jenny couldn't understand the words, but she could imagine what he was talking about. As the starman sat back the mother's expression shifted between wonderment and wariness.

The sky rumbled. Distant thunder promised forthcoming rain. Jenny glanced upward. 'Storm coming in.'

'*Aquí, aquí*,' muttered the old man, suddenly moving around. He started to unfurl a pile of thick canvas. Jenny leaned over to help him.

By that afternoon the temporary roof had been set in place over the pickup's bed. Thick clouds had accumulated threateningly overhead, but so far only a few drops had fallen.

The old man and the woman lay together beneath an old army blanket, resting peacefully. Jenny wondered if he was her father, or perhaps the father of the man driving the truck. Or maybe he was just a hitchhiker like themselves. Appearances could be deceiving.

Of all people she ought to know about that.

She held the baby in her arms, rocking it gently and cooing to it as it slept. The mother had finally agreed to hand the child over so she could get some rest herself. The baby moved slightly in its warm blanket, tiny hands reaching instinctively. Jenny cuddled it close, murmuring softly to it.

'*Probrecita*.'

'A new person is called a *probrecita*?'

She smiled across at him. The two of them were huddled together beneath another army blanket and he was very close to her. She no longer minded the closeness, no longer found the proximity disturbing.

'Only if they're Spanish and have a toothache. Otherwise they're called babies.'

'Can anyone have babies?'

'Just girls.'

'I did not mean that. I meant, any female. I understand your reproductive process. That information was presented clearly on the device that helped us to find your world.'

'You said "your" reproductive process. You don't have babies?'

'Not in the same sense as you. We are very long-lived, Jennyhayden, and much content with ourselves. The creation of a new person is a serious matter among us and is not taken lightly.'

'Same way with us. Well, most of the time, anyway.'

'You have a baby?'

'No. No babies. No dogs, no cats, no canary birds.'

'You were not married long enough?'

'No, it's more than that. Scott knew. I told him right away, as soon as we started getting serious. He understood. It didn't matter to him.' She tried to smile and failed. 'Just turned out I couldn't. Everybody can't do something. I was just one of those lucky ladies who can't . . .'

A loud crack of thunder interrupted her, went rolling off to the north. Lightning painted the underside of a cloud with light. Then the cloud and its companions opened up and the travelers found themselves journeying onward beneath a waterfall.

It rained all the way to Gallup, in northwestern New Mexico. Surprisingly, the old canvas kept the majority of it off, so they were almost dry when the pickup pulled in next to the railroad siding.

The old man raised the back flap and peered out. No yard men in sight. Probably all sitting in their shack drinking hot coffee, he thought. The long lines of boxcars trailed back into the rain, like ghosts.

There was a clash of couplings as the freight train lurched forward in front of him. He turned and waved into the darkness beneath the canvas. '*Vamanos*, hurry up! The train going west is moving. Go quickly now.'

Jenny and the starman climbed over the tailgate and stepped down into shallow mud. She led him toward the slowly accelerating train, searching the cars. The young mother followed behind while the old man stayed in the back of the truck with the child.

'Here!' Jenny indicated a boxcar whose door was slightly ajar. The starman grabbed it and shoved it aside, gave her a hand up and then followed.

Once they were safely aboard, the young woman tossed a bundle of material at them. 'Here, a blanket. It's dry.' As the train continued to pick up speed she began to fall behind. '*Vaya con dios.*'

'Good-bye, thank you!' Jenny leaned out and watched for as long as she was able. The young mother was still waving to them as the train picked up speed and moved off the siding out onto the main track.

'Close the door.' The starman nodded once, leaned his weight against it until it shut tight. Their haven thus secured from curious eyes, Jenny turned to inspect their surroundings as she wrung water out of her hair.

The interior of the boxcar was dry. Except for a few boxes and crates it was also empty, which explained why the door had been left unlocked. Nothing to steal.

Behind her, the starman sneezed.

153

'You'd better get out of those wet clothes. Maybe you can heal others by waving your fingers over 'em, but if you let that body get good and sick you may not be able to do anything for yourself.'

'Why get out of clothes?'

'The water'll chill your skin and make you do worse things than sneeze.'

'What is sneeze?' He did it again.

'That is "sneeze," and there'll be worse coming if you don't listen to me. I swear, you are the strangest blend of brains and stupidity I ever saw. Come on, like this.' She demonstrated what she wanted him to do by unbuttoning the top buttons of his shirt.

'We've got to get you warm. You know what pneumonia is?' He shook his head. 'No? Well you're liable to find out unless we get you dry in a hurry. It's not something that'd be much fun to study firsthand.' She continued working on his shirt. 'Come on, help me. You haven't got a damn thing I haven't seen a thousand times before.'

The starman just stood and let her do all the work. She finished with his shirt, then moved on to his shoes and pants. Finally he was standing in front of her, stark naked and utterly unself-conscious. To him she had merely removed the outer set of clothing, the one composed of artificial fibers.

She picked up the blanket and started wrapping it around him. He put out a hand to touch her gently in the hollow of her throat.

'You are wet also. You will not catch this pneumonia if you stay wet?'

She didn't know how to reply. 'I'm not immune to it, if that's what you mean.' They were touching and she was acutely conscious of the warmth of his body. 'I'm not going to catch cold, though.'

'Why not?'

'Well – because.'

'That is no reason.' She didn't stop him when he reached for the zipper on her windbreaker.

154

There was nothing unnatural about it, nothing at all. She knew every inch of that body. It was like the first time because he didn't know what to do or how to move, but the mechanism responded to her and he was a superb learner. Outside, the thunder rumbled and the train rattled on through the night and somehow it didn't seem to matter. Images and visions careened wildly through her mind and it was all perfectly wonderful.

Though she didn't think it was quite what Shakespeare had in mind when he wrote, 'There are more things in heaven and Earth than you've dreamed of, Horatio.'

It was calm by the time the helicopter touched down at the airfield. Clouds still hovered overhead, but the rain which had buffeted the chopper on its southward flight had moved off to the east.

Shermin jumped down and examined his surroundings, then started toward the hangar that loomed across the tarmac. Two guards flanked the entrance. Despite the fact that his helicopter had set down within punting range of their position, he still had to produce three separate pieces of identification before they would admit him.

Inside the hangar it was not calm. Soldiers and technicians were running, not walking, to their assigned stations. Desk and office equipment were being set in position, files full of papers placed atop the desks, telephone lines hooked up. All the activity conveyed the impression that something important was going on. It wasn't, not yet.

There were no reference points for Shermin in the organized chaos of the hangar. Then he spotted the major from Wisconsin. At about the same time, the officer noticed him standing forlornly near the doorway and crossed to greet him.

'Hi. I'm Bell, remember?'

'Sure I remember. Hasn't been that long. That's what's so crazy about this whole thing. Everything's happened so damn fast. How come they brought you all the way down?'

155

'Because I'm more or less familiar with what this is all about. I guess they figure the fewer who have any idea what's going on, the better.' He waved at the chamber behind them. 'As you can see, it's not slowing down. Oh, Mister Fox wanted you to know that he was delayed getting out of Washington. He'll be late arriving.'

'What's this all for? I didn't get all the details. After we lost them at the roadblock in Colorado I was told to report here. Looks like you're setting up for something major. No pun intended.'

Bell grinned politely. 'For the foreseeable future this is going to serve as a base of operations. Seems that while the rest of us have been running around trying to convince our visitor to give himself up quietly and with a minimum of fuss, intelligence has been doing its own work. They finally figured out that according to the speed and trajectory of the visitor's craft – I think we can stop referring to it as a hollow meteorite – it was originally headed for some-place in northeastern Arizona or northwest New Mexico. Since leaving Wisconsin in the company of Mrs Hayden, he's been heading straight here. You put one and one together, you come up with thoughts of some kind of rendezvous. The powers-that-be think his friends may try to send another meteor to pick him up. Make yourself at home.'

The major moved off to direct the installation of additional equipment. Shermin noticed a couple of white-coated lab techs hauling something glassy and complex toward the far side of the room. Curious, he pushed his way through the crowd toward them.

'Whatcha got?'

'Pathology supplies,' one of the techs replied with a grunt. 'Cryogenic suspension system elements. Stuff like that.'

'Uh-huh.' Tagging along behind, Shermin found himself in a screened-off section of the hangar where other techs were setting up additional gear. Three of them were very carefully unpacking an electron microscope. Another was busy at a hastily installed stainless steel sink, washing out

156

containers and glass beakers. Next to him a nurse was supervising the unloading of an impressive array of surgical instruments.

In the center of the room was a gleaming operating table equipped with leather straps. An electrician was working on the big mirrored light that hung over the table. Shermin stayed out of the man's way as he examined one of the leather straps.

'Welcome to planet Earth,' he murmured. No one overheard. They were too busy.

The clouds over northern Arizona had vanished eastward to reveal the desert night sky, alive with the stars city-dwellers only see on the bowls of planetariums. Train wheels rattled musically against the rails. Somewhere out in the barren mountains a coyote howled, the faint *yip-yip* rising and falling with comical speed.

Clad in his almost dry shirt, chinos, and shoes, the starman sat by the open door of the boxcar, staring out into the darkness. From time to time he would turn to check on Jenny. She slept soundly, rolled up in the cocoon of the old blanket and shielded from the wind by the little wall of empty crates and containers he had piled up around her.

The train whistle screamed, more for the engineer's amusement than out of necessity. In this country, even the sight of a steer on the tracks was an event. Jenny groaned, rolled over and stretched. Halfway through the stretch she opened her eyes, woke up, then turned over and stared at her silent companion.

'Where are we? What time is it?' She looked past him at the stark, moonlit countryside. 'At least the rain's stopped. We won't drown when we get out.'

'It isn't late,' he told her softly. 'Time passes swiftly when one is able to use it for contemplation.'

'Really?' She sat up, holding the blanket around her. 'And what have you been contemplating?'

'Various things.' He gestured outside. 'I think your

157

world is at its most attractive when both it and its inhabitants are at their quietest. I think we come to Winslow soon.'

'Why didn't you wake me?'

'I like to watch you sleep. That was also for contemplation. It must be an interesting state of being for an intelligent person to experience. I cannot experience it, I can only hypothesize what it must be like, but I enjoy watching you do it.' He hesitated before continuing. 'I do not know why. It is very strange. Adaptation works both ways. I was chosen explorer because I am very adaptable, more so than most of my kind. But the more time I spend in this body, the more I become like a planet Earth person. To me this is both an enjoyment and a danger.'

She shuffled around, trying to get comfortable on the hard floor. 'Do you have to go back? Isn't there some way you could stay here, like a permanent observer or something?' Still holding the blanket around her, she crawled over to be next to him. He reached out and touched her lightly.

'No. I must go back. Even if I could remain in this body, I could not stay in this mind.'

She smiled and shook her head. 'I don't understand.'

'I miss my own kind. This is not my world, not my home. Not my way of life. I was not designed for it. My adaptation to your form is as temporary as my adaptation to your ways. Spirit does not follow shape.' He looked away from her, back out into the night. When he spoke again there was a new solemnity in his voice.

'There is something I must tell you. I do not know how such things are said, so I will simply say it. I gave you a baby tonight.'

She inhaled sharply. 'No. That's impossible. Even if you were human it'd be impossible. I can't have a child. I told you, I've been to a half dozen doctors and they all say the same thing. It's not a matter of choice; it's a matter of bad plumbing.'

'This is outside their experience.'

158

She thought back to what had happened earlier that evening. 'Well, I don't think any of them would argue that one with you, but still . . .'

'Believe what I tell you, Jennyhayden. When you were shot by the policeman, I healed you. When our car struck the big truck filled with gas you would have burned but I prevented it. Both times I repaired your body. This time I fixed earlier damage. It was not difficult. To you your system may seem terribly complicated. To me it is no more so than the innards of this train.

'You will have a baby. A boy baby. Not a *probrecita*. I was very careful. It is a matter of careful engineering.'

She didn't know what to do, how to react. She would have laughed if not for the blatant absurdity of what he was saying. There was too much warmth surrounding her for her to scream. So she just sat and stared.

'He will be human, this child of your dead husband. The only genes involved are his and yours. But at the same time he will also be my – new person. Offspring. Baby.' He nodded to himself. 'Yes, baby. That word is best. He will be mine because I engineered those genes. *That* is difficult to do, but not impossible. Biochemistry. There is much about your own makeup, your own DNA, that you do not understand. Much that is not used properly by your bodies. There are parts of your genetic code that are blank, like pieces of paper. I wrote on the blank pieces. That part of the baby will be me.' He turned to look deeply into her eyes.

'There is one thing I can do. If you do not want this baby, say so now and I will stop it. I can do that as painlessly as I started it. It will be as if it never was.'

She considered quietly, realizing that here was something Important she was going to have to deal with even if she didn't quite understand.

'He'll look normal? Like any other human baby? Like the one belonging to the woman who gave us the blanket?'

'Like any normal human child, yes,' he assured her. 'Except that it will not hurt when it gets its teeth. I fixed that, too.'

Now she did laugh, softly, out of amazement. 'I've had some surprises dumped on me early in the morning, but this . . .' She took a deep breath and looked past him, tilting her head back to stare up into the brilliantly clear sky. 'Tell me, which of those is your star? Your sun? Can you see it from here?'

'Why do you ask?'

'I'll want to show him where his other father came from – if he'll believe me.'

'When he has matured, he will understand.' He searched the heavens. 'There – no, wait – over to the right a little, near that bright grouping low on the horizon. Your atmosphere is so thick and variable that sometimes it is hard to be certain. But if you look hard you can see.'

She strained her eyes. 'Where? There are so many.'

He pointed to a saddle between two hills. 'Down there. See it? Just above that notch in the rocks and slightly to the right. It is not very bright from here, but it is much like your own star, though older. As our world is older. As we are.'

'I see it. I see it.'

Intervening hills cut off her view as the train swept around a wide curve. Pink light began to wash out the sky anyway, a sure indication that they were coming into a good-size town.

'You'd better get dressed,' he told her, leaning out the opening to look past the distant engine. 'I think we must be coming into Winslow.'

Jenny ignored her clothing to stare at the city lights that were growing steadily brighter ahead of them. She frowned. 'I didn't think Winslow would be so big. 'Course, the geography of the southwest isn't exactly my specialty. I have a tough time finding my way around Madison. I just hope to God we're on the right train.'

'Something is the matter?'

'I hope not, but those lights are *so* bright. And there are so many of them.' Now she turned away and retreated back into the boxcar to get dressed. He was watching her

160

again, but she no longer minded his stare.

An hour passed before the starman cautiously slid the door aside and peered out into the railyard. The train had been at rest for some time now and still no one had come along to check the empty cars. He hopped out, reached back up and in to help Jenny down.

They started walking toward the bright glow in the sky. 'There are a lot of tracks.'

'Maybe Winslow's a major siding. That's where they put trains that are waiting to go someplace else. A lot of small towns are like that; a grocery, a couple of bars, gas station at each end, maybe a cafe – and twenty acres of track.'

They crossed a parking lot. 'There's a building up ahead. Looks like it might be a station.' Her stomach was churning. This didn't feel right. A town like Winslow shouldn't rate a station.

But that's what the building turned out to be; a terminal, and much too big to belong to any town the size of Winslow. Though empty of people at this early morning hour, it was brightly lit and well cared for. A single sign above the double doorway said it all:

LAS VEGAS

'Las Vegas! We were on the right train but we didn't get off in time. We went past Winslow. Way past.'

'What?'

'Don't you see? We've come too far. We're in the wrong town.' She glanced at her watch. 'It's still the middle of the night. We've got time – I hope.'

A couple of porters appeared on the station platform. They were busy talking and didn't notice the man and woman standing down on the tracks. Jenny grabbed the starman's arm and hustled him around the side, into an empty storage alcove.

She cautioned him to be quiet and listened to the conversation above, ignoring the stench of oil and grease.

161

Eventually the two porters went away, probably back into the station to wait for customers. She whispered to her patient companion.

'We've gone about three hundred miles past Winslow, but we're still all right. All we've got to do is rent a car. With any kind of luck we can still make it back to Winslow before dawn. That means we've got to go into town. Just try not to be conspicuous, okay? Last thing we want is to attract any attention.'

He nodded, extracted the baseball cap from his back pocket and placed it on his head. He put it on back to front, the way Scott used to wear it. When he saw the anguished expression this produced he hasted to correct it.

'I am sorry. I was not being thoughtful.'

'Never mind. Just leave it like that, please?' He nodded understandingly. She led him up a service ladder onto the side of the passenger platform. There was no sign of the porters or anyone else. 'Come on.'

They hitched a ride downtown and the cheerful lineman dropped them off on Fremont Street.

'Thanks for the lift,' Jenny told him.

'Hey, no sweat. I been broke in this town myself. That was ten years ago. Had to get a job to eat and ended up staying. Not a bad place to live. Not everybody here's a crook or a conman, y'know.'

'Right,' said the starman, giving the lineman the thumbs-up.

'Take care, you two, and hang onto your money.' He waved as he drove off into the glitter.

The starman was absolutely delighted: with the flashing lights, the rippling neon art, the screams of excited winners at the nickel slots, and the echoing bark of the crap-table croupiers. One small casino had a live barker stationed out front, standing and gesturing wildly beneath a sign that spelled out in explosive red and yellow—

WIN WIN WIN GIANT JACKPOT $500,000!!!

162

'Half-a-million dollars, folks. Who's gonna take it home? Hit the giant jackpot and your troubles are over! Come on, friends, it's burning a hole in our pockets and it might as well end up in yours. Free drinks and dollar ninety-eight steak dinner, it's all on us folks!'

The starman looked back over his shoulder at the frantic pitchman until he was swallowed up by the crowd, then down at Jenny. 'Define "giant jackpot."'

'A giant jackpot is a lot of money,' she explained absently. She was searching the smaller doorways. There should be several rent-a-car places scattered among the casinos and hotels. She'd always heard that people who came to Vegas often ended up selling their cars to pay their debts. That meant they'd need some way of returning home.

Sure enough, a modest sign above a door across the street was flashing:

RENT-A-WRECK – OPEN 24 HOURS, 365 DAYS A YEAR

The starman was still working on her definition of giant jackpot. 'Lot of money? Like geetus, bread, an arm and a leg?'

Jenny led him across the street, watching the traffic while hunting through her purse. 'Yeah, that's right, but we don't have time to fool around with slot machines and stuff. If we're going to get back to Winslow on time then we . . .' She stopped as she stepped up onto the sidewalk. 'Hey, where the hell's my wallet?'

'What's wrong?'

She was pawing anxiously through her purse, shoving aside lipstick, comb and brush, safety pins, a stubby pen, finding everything except what she wanted.

'My wallet, my credit cards. Everything, gone. I – oh my God.'

She remembered: Elmo's, back in Colorado. The phone call, setting her wallet down next to the telephone, the waitress telling her where the starman had gone. Rushing out of the booth and leaving the wallet behind.

That was it, then. It was the end.

She dug through the detritus one last time, found only a quarter, two pennies, and a postage stamp. She turned to face him, stricken. 'I left my wallet in a restaurant in Colorado. I'm sorry. I'm so damn sorry.'

'Is all right.'

'No, is *not* all right! I don't think you understand. We have no money, no credit cards, nothing. No way to pay for a car. I've ruined everything. I could wire Mrs Gilman for some money, but even if I could get ahold of her it would never get here in time. The banks back home are closed and nobody here's going to loan me any money without some identification.'

He took the quarter from her hand, inspected it briefly. 'Is all right,' he told her again. 'I watched as we walked.' He stepped past her, crossed back to the casino with the barker out front. Numbly, she followed.

Through the mirrored entryway, into the back of the casino, past the roulette wheels and crap tables he led her, finally halting in front of a line of quarter slots that were somewhat isolated from the rest of the late-night action. Jenny's temporary shock dissipated as she realized what he had in mind. She had a clear memory of what he'd done to a certain recalcitrant Coke machine, but it was still a dangerous ploy. Yet she had no alternatives to propose.

She could still help, though, and made him wait until the floorman had walked past. He hadn't so much as glanced in their direction.

'Now,' she whispered to her companion.

The starman dropped the quarter into the slot, pulled the handle on the side of the machine. He watched the three wheels rotate for a moment, then put a hand on each side of the metal box. A faint humming noise was barely audible above the whirr and clank of the machinery. A pale luminosity emanated from the glass window. The wheels stopped one at a time, left to right. A bar, another bar, and – a lemon.

Jenny slumped. She'd had only the one quarter. She was about to turn away when he seemed to nudge the machine ever so slightly. The lemon struggled with itself and gave way to a third bar. Coins began to pour out of the hole at the bottom of the one-armed bandit, which was ringing wildly.

Someone had left a small plastic bucket atop a nearby machine. It was one of those cheap ice buckets that lower-class hotels and motels supply to every room. Grabbing the bucket she stuck it under the orifice, but it still wasn't enough to hold the seemingly endless stream of quarters. She dropped to hands and knees and began picking them off the carpet.

'That's a handy little talent you've got there,' she told him, 'but let's spread it around a little. We'd better move to another casino. See, they get curious if you hit too many jackpots in one place. Besides, we'll only need another couple like this one to . . . hey?'

She rose, cradling the heavy bucket in both arms. Her companion was nowhere to be seen. He could have wandered off anywhere, into a floor show or worse, back out onto the street. She tried to see over the ranked machines, wishing she was taller, when suddenly all hell broke loose. Whistles were blowing, sirens wailing, bells shrilling madly. Above everything a recorded voice could be heard repeating over and over, with just the right mixture of hysteria and delight:

GIANT JACKPOT GIANT JACKPOT GIANT JACKPOT!!!

'Oh no.' She forced her way through the gathering crowd, ignoring the quarters that spilled from the ice bucket.

Sure enough, there he was, standing glibly in front of the oversized slot machine, wondering at the sudden commotion and bewilderedly accepting the congratulations of enthusiastic spectators. In the big glass window in the middle of the machine five sevens were lined up neatly in a row like so many toy soldiers. People packed in tight around him: women in beehive hairdos, men in slick suits whose true status was revealed by the state of their shoes, all manners of hangers-on who believed proximity to such luck might bring them a little of their own.

Jenny tried to reach him but it was slow going through the dense crowd. From a side door marked MANAGER a neatly dressed middle-aged man emerged. He was trailed by an older man carrying a camera.

They were met by another individual almost as big as the two of them put together who had 'Security' written all over him.

'What happened?' the manager asked quietly.

'One buck!' The security man was shaking his head in disbelief. 'One lousy buck. He changed four quarters for a silver dollar and hit for half a million.'

The manager digested this as he gave orders to his PR man. 'Get plenty of shots.' To the security bull, 'Is he a mechanic?' The photographer moved around them to do his job while the two older men considered the still growing crowd.

'I can't make him but – I don't know. It's weird, but I'd swear I've seen his face before. There's something familiar about it that I can't put my finger on.'

'What?'

'I don't know. I guess if I've seen it it's got to be in the weekly casino updates.'

'Well go and find it, and try to make it some time this month.' The security man vanished like a wraith. The manager sighed and began making his way through the crowd. Of all the duties attendant upon running a Las Vegas casino, the task he was about to perform was the least pleasant.

The publicity man was grabbing one picture after another, doing his job, making sure to get plenty of full-face shots. The latter were for the police, not the newspapers. To the manager the lucky winner looked concerned, but not nervous. A mechanic, no matter how carefully he tried to hone his act, would be nervous.

166

The starman was relieved to see a familiar face pushing toward him through the crowd. 'Jennyhayden!'

'Hang on!' A moment later she was standing next to him. There was nothing she could do about the photographer, so she ignored the repeated blasts from his flash. It didn't matter. By the time any pictures could be developed and recognized, their subject would be long gone.

If they didn't waste anymore time, that is.

'You went and did it, didn't you?'

'I did wrong?'

She stared at the five sevens in a row, saw the big '5' beneath it followed by a string of fat zeroes, and shook her head. 'It's not exactly that you did wrong. It's kind of hard to explain . . .'

Before she could do so the manager joined them, introduced himself with a big smile, and insisted on having formal pictures taken with the lucky winner in front of the traitorous machine. The crowd dispersed along with the initial excitement, taking with them a little fresh hope. If the quiet young man could get rich in one night, so could they. Within the casino the action intensified, the levers of one-armed bandits were pulled with a bit more panache.

The manager delayed as long as possible before handing over the thick manila envelope. He was smiling because it was his duty to smile, but he was anything but happy.

'That's twenty-five thousand in cash and the casino's check for the balance. I suggest you sign it first chance you get. Congratulations.' Before letting go of the envelope he glanced one final time toward the back of the room. His security chief was standing outside the office, shaking his head sadly. With a sigh the manager let loose of the money.

The starman accepted it gracefully. He displayed none of the feverish excitement so typical of big winners and only succeeded in piquing the manager's curiosity further.

'Thank you.'

Loath to loose sight of the winner, much less the half

million, the manager made a last pitch for the casino's services. 'That's a lot of money to be carrying around, sir.' He nodded toward the milling crowd of less fortunate gamblers. 'There are those who put their trust in stronger weapons than lady luck. They watch and wait for a big winner like yourself and then jump him once he's back out on the street.' He gestured with one hand and the chief of security hurried to join them.

'Our security people will be glad to escort you safely back to your hotel. Or if you wish, we'll be glad to keep your winnings here in our safe until you can make arrangements to have the whole sum transferred to your home town bank when it opens later this morning. You might want to avail yourself further of our facilities, try your hand at roulette or baccarat. Refreshments for both of you are on the house, of course, for as long as you'd like to stay and play.'

'No thanks,' Jenny said quickly. 'We don't have far to go. We'll be all right. Thanks anyway.'

'Good-bye.' Politely, the starman shook hands with the manager. 'Yeah, Cornhuskers.'

The manager watched them leave. Not only was he unhappy over the payout, he was an Oklahoma fan.

His security chief stood on his right and strained to remember where he'd seen that face before. Because he had, and not long ago. He was sure of it.

But 'sure' ain't reason enough for calling the cops, and there's no publicity in Vegas worse than mistreating an honest winner.

The night clerk at the car rental agency didn't blink when they put down cash for the one-week rental. The starman pulled cleanly out of the garage in a new Cadillac Eldorado and guided the big coupe out of town under Jenny's direction. They had a new car full of gas, money in their pockets, and a good map, and all was right with the world. If it would only stay that way for another few hours, Jenny prayed silently.

It doesn't take long to get out of Las Vegas. Before long

they were on Highway 93 heading southeast. The first sign they encountered was reassuring.

KINGMAN 75
FLAGSTAFF 256
WINSLOW 292

Jenny used the power control to lower her seat but she still couldn't relax, unable to believe that they'd made a clean getaway. The digital speedometer showed a reading of sixty-eight.

'Slow down.'

'Why? We have gone faster than this before.'

'I know, but that's when we were trying to get away from people who were chasing us. Keep 'er at sixty and we've got it knocked. The last thing we want now is some zealous highway patrolman pulling us over for exceeding the speed limit.'

'Whatever you say, Jennyhayden.' Obediently he eased off the accelerator until the readout on the dash read sixty. The road dipped and rose, twisted around curves and straightened out across open desert, and the speedometer reading never wavered.

Nine

Fox led Bell and a gaggle of other underlings into the modified hangar. Some of them were in uniforms, others in civvies. The level of activity within the building had become less frenetic as personnel were assigned to and assumed various duty stations. Hands danced over instruments and fine-tuned sensitive equipment while eyes were locked on video screens. Everyone was busy, and everyone was waiting for something to happen.

'. . . after ground units have secured an outer perimeter of fifty miles,' Fox was saying, 'choppers from the local air cav unit will search the designated area in quarter-mile grids.' He broke off as Shermin emerged from behind a movable partition. 'That's all for now, gentlemen. I'd like updates every fifteen minutes, please, regardless of developments.' Several of the men and women nodded before all went their separate ways. The security director moved to intercept his advisor.

'Good, you're here. Wasn't sure you'd make it before me. I hear the weather up north is lousy.'

'We missed it.' Shermin didn't sound particularly pleased to see his employer. He glanced back at the screened-off area. 'What the hell's that all about?'

Fox pursed his lips and formed his response carefully. 'You're a man of some scientific accomplishment. Surely you know an emergency autopsy room when you see one.'

'With leather tie-downs? Who's the pathologist? Torquemada? Besides, he isn't dead.'

'Behave yourself, Mark. We need to be ready for

anything. There are no guidelines for what's happening out here. Even if we take him alive, we don't want him hurting himself. Or anyone else, either. I read your report on what happened in Colorado. The power to preserve can also be used to destroy.'

'I love the way you impugn motives to something you know nothing about.'

'It's part of my job.' Fox nodded toward the portable surgery. 'As for that, it isn't all my doing, you know. I'm just running the field operation. My orders come from Washington.'

'Yeah, I know. You're only following orders.'

Fox's expression narrowed but he chose to say nothing more. Instead, he beckoned for Shermin to follow as he crossed to a wall where a huge map of the United States had been posted. An acetate overlay had been pinned to the map.

Someone had drawn on the acetate with red and blue grease pencils. A smooth red line ran from the left of the map, over the Pacific, across the northern tier of states, to come to an end in Wisconsin. A line of dotted red broke away from the solid just above the state of Washington. It curved down over the western part of the country, crossing Nevada and Arizona to finally peter out over Old Mexico.

The single blue line was not smooth. It zigged and zagged its way southward from Wisconsin, heading toward the Four Corners area where Utah, Colorado, Arizona, and New Mexico meet. The line was solid as far south as Grand Junction, Colorado. From there it became a dotted squiggle that wormed its way hesitantly down into Mexico.

The dotted red and blue lines intersected just west of Flagstaff, Arizona.

A young army technician stood next to the map. 'Is this your latest update?' Fox asked him.

The man nodded, indicated the map. 'According to NORAD his original course and rate of descent – we can't plot the latter on a two-dimensional map, of course – would have brought him down in this area, near Winslow

171

and the Painted Desert. None of that is certain, of course, but the projection is the best one the computers have given us so far. Unless we receive new data I don't expect it to change.'

As Fox was mulling this over in his mind they were rejoined by Major Bell. He smiled briefly at Shermin.

'I see,' Fox murmured. 'Anything else?'

'No sir.'

Bell spoke up, sounded almost apologetic. 'I've got something, sir. The Cobra guys were asking about ammunition. I told them to hold off loading until I had a chance to talk to you. How do you want to handle that? We could take on blanks alternating with tracers.'

Fox shook his head. 'No. Helicopter attack units will carry live ammo at all times. This is to be treated like a combat mission.'

'Whatever you say, sir.' Bell looked somber as he walked away.

Fox took a last look at the map before turning and heading for a door marked 'Men' near the back of the room. Shermin dogged his heels.

'Listen, Mister Fox, I want to be a team player and all that, but there's a little something I'd like to call to your attention.'

Fox whirled on him. 'Don't bother, Shermin. I know what you're going to say, and what I don't need from you is a lecture on morality. Not now. I've got the joint chiefs of staff, the heads of the FBI and the CIA, and the president himself all breathing down my neck and wanting updates on the situation every five minutes while I'm going crazy trying to organize this mission in something halfway like a sensible fashion. I haven't got the time or the inclination to listen to a lot of bathos about understanding between peoples and extending the hand of friendship across the reaches between the stars. My job is to ensure the peace and tranquility of this country, and that's damn well what I intend to do.

'If this whatever he is would just turn himself in,

everything would work out fine and dandy. But he hasn't done so and he shows no inclination to do so. I'm not going to make any bad jokes about illegal aliens because it's not a funny situation. This creature has demonstrated its abilities and powers on more than one occasion. We're charged with taking it into custody before it can harm anyone. I hardly need remind you we have a reliable report that it pointed a forty-five caliber automatic at a policeman up in Colorado.'

'The cops were trying to run him off the road. He might have felt just a little bit threatened.'

'That doesn't justify pulling a gun. That's not what I'd call a "friendly" gesture. One more incident like that might result in a couple of civilian deaths. If that happens I'm gone. You understand? Gone, finished, and my staff with me. I hardly need remind you that includes yourself, Shermin.'

Shermin listened stolidly to Fox's recitation, then removed a cigar from his pocket and began peeling it slowly and deliberately.

'All right. Morality aside and discounting that state trooper's story, which we have no way of verifying, what's he done to warrant loading up search helicopters with live ammunition?'

'You're a hard one to convince, aren't you? All right, you want more?' Fox ticked off the points on the tips of his fingers. 'He's run at every opportunity to turn himself in and he's kidnapped a local woman.'

'She says not.'

'Sure she does, during one hurried telephone conversation with him maybe holding a gun or heaven knows what else up against her neck. Following which he crashed the both of them into a jackknifed gas tanker and lights up half of southern Colorado, after which he reveals his command of a supposedly defensive force-field or something like that in order to escape. That's *your* report I'm quoting, not some uneducated trooper's. Oh, he's harmless, all right. And don't forget his initial overflight of the nuclear sub base up at Bremerton. He's probably carrying that information around with him, too.'

'That's nonsense! His flight path just happened to take him over upstate Washington. There are so damn many military bases in this country you can't fly anywhere without running into one sooner or later. You think he crossed interstellar space just to spy on our primitive weapons capabilities?'

Fox's reply was deadly serious. 'That's what we have to ask him, isn't it? We *have* to ask him. Nicely if possible, but ask him we will.'

'What the hell ever happened to good manners.' Shermin didn't try to hide his anger or his frustration. 'We invited him here!'

Fox sighed. He was very tired, Shermin saw, which was understandable considering the pressure he was under. Maybe it was affecting his judgment. Shermin wanted to be understanding, but he could not.

'I don't have time for this, Shermin.'

'I'm trying to make a point.'

'So am I. First, nothing about this encounter is as cut and dried as we'd like it to be. So far we haven't been able to get in touch with this creature, much less figure out what he wants here.

'Second, you make a great show of being a rebel and iconoclast within the department, but the facts are that you're still a Class G-II public servant, with all the considerable perks and emoluments pertaining thereto. Your job is to provide opinions *when* solicited, give advice *when* it's asked for. Any time that becomes too heavy a burden you can go back to Cornell or wherever the hell we found you and try making it on a professor's salary. I've seen your condo, your Jaguar, and your state-of-the-art video setup, Shermin. I don't think you're all that anxious to return to the wonderfully poverty-stricken independence of academia, are you?' Fox took no pleasure in Shermin's lack of a reply. The security director wasn't the type to gloat, and he needed the scientist's advice.

174

'I thought as much. Now shape up or get off this base. Whine all you want, but keep it to yourself.'

Fox had more to say but he was interrupted by the arrival of Major Bell. The major carried a single printout.

'What've you got, Bell?' Fox glanced warningly at Shermin, but the advisor held his peace. 'Something worthwhile, I hope? We're overdue.'

'Can't be certain, Mister Fox, but there's been a possible sighting in Las Vegas.'

'Las Vegas! How the hell did they get that far without being spotted by our people?'

'I don't know, sir, but the report has them leaving town and heading east. They're probably still coming this way.'

Fox relaxed slightly. 'So our initial assumptions are still valid. Good. I'd hate to have to pick up this whole crew and set up all over again someplace like Barstow. But why Vegas?'

'Maybe they took the roundabout route to try and throw us off the track, sir,' Bell suggested. 'Orders?'

'Set up a field command post in Winslow. Keep it as small as possible, minimum staff. We don't want to alarm the locals.' He turned to Shermin. 'You'd better get over there too. Providing, of course, you're still a member of the team. You are, aren't you?'

'Yes sir, Mister Fox, sir,' Shermin said tightly.

'All right then. Get moving. You may find something worth seeing. And get rid of that damn cigar.' He pulled the unlit stogie out of Shermin's hand and tossed it to the floor before resuming his foray to the men's room.

Shermin ground his teeth and stared at the security director's retreating back. Good soldier that he was, Bell waited patiently nearby and said nothing.

The Eldorado's ride was smooth and relaxing as it bore through the night east of Flagstaff. The starman drove with the window down, luxuriating in the cool, fresh air.

'What time is it?'

Jenny indicated the digital clock located in the dash.

175

'You can see for yourself. A little after four. We ought to be coming up on that place called Rimmy Jim's any time now.' She smiled at him. 'We're going to make it. Close, but we're going to make it. You're going home.'

He didn't react and she couldn't interpret his expression. Not that that would necessarily be a true reflection of his feelings anyway, she reminded herself.

'You want to go home, don't you?'

'Yes, of course. But because I want to go home does not mean I cannot also be sorry to leave, does it?'

'No, I guess not.' She leaned forward to peer through the windshield, staring up at the stars. 'What's it like up there, where you come from?'

'It is beautiful. Not like this. Differently beautiful. I think it would make you little bit jumpy.' She grinned at that. 'To us it is hard to imagine living anyplace else. There is only one method of communication, one system of law, one people. And there is no war and no hunger and the strong don't victimize the helpless. We are very ordered and controlled and civilized, and that in itself can be most beautiful.

'But at the same time, we have lost something.' He glanced over at her. 'Your race is so young, so very much alive. Where there exists the excitement of youth and immaturity there is also drama. Our existence is not so – dramatic. Everything here is so different. Even the way in which your bodies perceive existence is different. I will miss that, just as I will miss cooks and Cornhuskers and the singing and dancing and eating. And other things, many of which you take for granted. Your mornings are an example. Morning on my home is very ordered, very predictable. Yours is irregular and surprising. Best of all is its smell.' He inhaled deeply of the sweet desert air.

'Different every time. How wonderful to be able to smell a different morning just by travelling from one place to another. One of the great wonders of your world is its variety.'

'That's called "sagebrush,"' Jenny told him, a bit

overwhelmed by his explanation. 'It grows in the desert.'

'Do you know what you have here?' he asked her suddenly, displaying more enthusiasm than he had since she'd known him. 'What kind of world this can be, what kind of people you can be? So much potential! So much ability and talent, and so much of it wasted on the frivolous, the unjust, and the primitive. You can be more than friends. You can be, in time, equals.' He sighed and she felt the emotion go straight through her.

'You have so far to go, and yet I will still miss this beautiful place, your planet Earth. You have not yet fouled it beyond hope. There is still a chance for your people to realize their inherent potential.'

'How? What can we do? What should we do?'

'You will have to grow up,' he told her quietly. 'There was an entertainment on the video communicator, the television, in the motel where we met the Cornhuskers. I watched it only briefly but it was better than most of what I watched. One of the entertainers was speaking to another. He said, "It is time to put away childish things." That is what your people must try to do, Jennyhayden. You have been playing with childish things for too long now, and it is time to put them away.'

She sat silently and wished he would keep talking, but now it was his turn to reflect and consider.

A sign hove into view, briefly afire in the Cadillac's lights.

METEOR CRATER – 3 MI

They slowed, followed the signs off the Interstate onto a narrow road that led south into the desert.

Before the desert was Rimmy Jim's, and it was closed. Even the gas station was dark and sealed. Only the Crater Cafe remained open in hopes of providing sustenance and succor to those occasional travelers passing through late at night.

The Caddy rolled into the dirt parking lot. As he exited, the starman stumbled once and had to catch his balance on

177

the front of the car. Jenny said nothing but felt a pang of concern. She'd never seen him miss a step before. It was clear he was growing rapidly weaker.

'Are you all right?' she finally asked.

'A little bit – tired. This near to the end of the time frame my control over this body is beginning to weaken.'

'Can you make it the rest of the way?'

'I think so.' He looked skyward, searching. 'They will be here soon. Then I will become myself again and all will be well.'

The interior of the cafe was given over, not surprisingly, to the single sight that supported the town. There were dozens of shots of the huge crater taken from every conceivable angle. Some were washed-out old color prints that must have dated from the forties. A couple of free-standing shelves proffered the usual plethora of tourist knickknacks, each incorporating the crater motif. There were Meteor Crater ashtrays, salt-and-pepper shakers, plates, pennants, bumper stickers, and so on, none of them made in the state of Arizona. The only genuine articles of local manufacture were scraps of petrified wood, from boxes full of fragments to expensive polished bookends, that had been gleaned from the borders of the nearby national monument. Geologic kitsch.

There were also 'Genuine Meteorites.' Tektites, though they looked like plain old rocks to Jenny.

When they entered it rang a bell somewhere in the kitchen. The manager, night cook, and waiter emerged to greet them. He was more cheerful and awake than anyone had a right to be at four o'clock in the morning.

'Hi, folks. What'll it be?'

'Dutch apple pie?' asked the starman hopefully.

The night cook shook his head apologetically. 'Sorry, not today. That was Monday. How about some nice cherry cobbler? Only as old as last night, which means it's still fresh.'

'That'll be fine,' Jenny told him.

'With whipped cream,' her companion added.

178

'Health nut, huh? You got it, bub. Comin' right up.' He vanished back into the kitchen.

Jenny and the starman took seats at one of the empty tables. 'How long does it take to get to the crater from here?' she called out to the cook.

He was back in minutes with their order. 'Driving? Not long. Five or six minutes is all. Come early to watch the sunrise over the crater, huh?' Before either of them could reply he went on. 'Not too many folks do that. They don't know what they're missing. Gives you a real primeval feelin', standing there watching the sun come up over the crater wall. That's what that crazy artist feller who's making another crater nearby into a work of art says, anyway. Me, I've seen it enough times not to be surprised by anything that happens out here.'

Wait around a few minutes, Jenny thought at him.

'This way you beat the heat, too.' He set the plates down in front of them, spoke to the starman. 'I want you to try this cherry cobbler with an open mind. If you don't like it, you don't have to pay for it.'

The starman dipped into the plate, using a fork this time, but there was nothing of the joy that had appeared on his face before, when he'd had that first bite of apple pie.

Jenny noticed his disappointment, was quick to say, 'It's delicious.'

'My wife made it.'

'It's very good,' said the starman, taking his cue from Jenny.

Content now, the cook returned to his kitchen to get ready for the morning breakfast rush. He prided himself on having the grill and everything else ready when the morning shift showed up.

Jenny picked at her cobbler. 'Tell me something. Do you have – a wife or somebody, up there?'

'No. It is different with us. Hard to explain. More a matter of hard physics than soft relationships. But I have many friends.'

'I see. I wish . . .'

179

'What?' He looked back at her out of that oh-so-familiar face. But the mind directing those eyes was not familiar. It functioned in ways she couldn't begin to imagine. If she'd been expecting some kind of gesture, kind words or an emotional confession, it wasn't forthcoming.

Stupid, she told herself. She dug angrily at her cobbler. What kind of fool was she? He hadn't the faintest idea what she was feeling or what she was waiting for, and it was insane of her to expect him to react in anything like a recognizable manner.

'Nothing.' On impulse, she reached out and covered one of his hands with her own. He stared back at her uncertainly, wanting to react in a way that would please her but not having the slightest idea how to do so.

The screen door banged against the jamb as it swung wide to admit a sergeant in the khaki-colored uniform of the Arizona Department of Public Safety. He was young for a sergeant, Jenny thought.

He did not sit down, did not call out an order. Instead he made a quick survey of the cafe's interior before his gaze settled on her. 'Evening, folks. That your Eldorado outside?'

She didn't reply. Instead, she pushed aside a curtain and looked out the window.

The parking lot was full of police cars.

Ten

Shermin found himself watching the sky as he turned off the Interstate. The bowl of the heavens had changed color, fading from pure black to a cold cobalt blue. Sun would be up soon. Then they'd have some answers.

How badly did he want them?

He pulled into the lot outside the cafe and parked, noting the number of patrol cars drawn up in a circle around the building. Like Indians attacking the wagon train, he thought, except that that was an old Hollywood myth. Real Indians had never done anything like that. They'd had too much sense to ride in circles around a heavily fortified position.

But in this case it looked like the battle was already over.

He climbed out and headed for the modest structure. A state trooper immediately intercepted him.

'Sorry sir. Cafe's closed.'

Shermin flashed his credentials. The trooper examined them intently for a moment, then tipped his hat and stepped aside. 'Sorry sir. Go right on in.'

Jenny Hayden and her male companion sat at a window table, the remains of some dessert still sitting in front of them. The bemused night cook would have taken the plates away if the sergeant hadn't politely prevented him from doing so. He'd been told to stay back in the kitchen, out of the way, and he'd complied. But they couldn't keep him from staring curiously out into his own restaurant.

And they'd seemed like such a nice young couple, too, he mused.

The sergeant looked up as Shermin entered. The science

181

advisor took in the souvenirs, the pictures on the walls, and the couple sitting silently nearby. Then he crossed to the sergeant and showed his identification for the second time.

'I'd like to talk to these people alone, officer.'

The sergeant looked at the couple seated next to the wall, then back at Shermin. 'All right, sir. I'll be outside if you need me.' He headed for the door, paused to glance back. 'Oh, George Fox just called in on the radio. Said to tell you that they're on their way over and for you to hold the fort for a couple of minutes.'

'I think I can handle things. Thank you, sergeant.' The officer closed the door behind him.

Now that he was alone in the room with the visitor, save for the woman who'd been accompanying him and one puzzled cook, Shermin found that he was trembling slightly.

Stop that, he ordered himself. That won't do anything any good. He desperately wanted a cigar but forebore from lighting up out of fear it might be harmful to the visitor. There was so much they didn't know, so much that could only be inferred.

He walked over to the table. Both of them were watching his approach warily. He tried to sound as reassuring as possible.

'I'm Mark Shermin from SETI – the Search for Extra-terrestrial Intelligence.'

'Tell me,' said the figure seated across from Jenny Hayden, 'have you found any?'

Shermin was taken aback. He'd come expecting anything but humor. 'I think so. SETI is kind of a semigovernmental agency.'

'Like you're kind of a semigovernment representative?' the woman said.

He smiled at her. 'Mrs Hayden, I – we talked on the phone. I have your wallet for you, by the way.'

'Just missed me, hmm?'

'Yes. I wish you'd stayed in that restaurant just a little while longer. We could have – I, this is such a—' He was trying to talk sense without taking his eyes off her companion,

182

and it wasn't easy. The replication was astounding. He'd seen the pictures of Scott Hayden and it was hard to believe that was him, sitting quietly on the other side of the table. It wasn't, of course. It wasn't even human.

To be a good scientist requires the ability to readily suspend disbelief. Mark Shermin had it in quantity, but he was having a hard time ignoring the evidence of his senses.

He sat down next to them. 'Mind if I sit down? This is a very special moment for me and I'm afraid I'm not handling it very well. There are so many questions I'd like to ask, I hardly know where to start. You know, you dream about having your life's greatest wish fulfilled, and then when it happens, you don't know what to do with it. I – is there anything I can do for you?'

Jenny stared hard at him. 'You can leave him alone, you can let him go.'

'I can't. Really. I'm sorry. It's out of my hands. You must understand that I'm just a consultant, a minor functionary. I can only give advice, advice which can be casually ignored and often is. I'm not one of the people who makes decisions. Never was. Those people will be here soon, I'm afraid.' He turned to face the visitor. 'Is it – are you supposed to meet someone here? Is that it?'

'Yes. Friends.'

How calm he is, Shermin thought. Surely he's seen the police cars outside, ringing the restaurant. He must know that he's trapped. But he wasn't acting like a trapped man.

Well, why should he? He wasn't. A man, that is.

Jenny spoke anxiously. 'There isn't much time. Please . . .'

Shermin seemed not to hear her. 'Why here? Why the crater? I know it's an obvious off-world landmark, but there are others. Is it because it's familiar to your people from previous visits? There's a lot of speculation that we've been visited before. Have your people been here before now?'

'Yes. Before. But not in person. Machines have come and probed and returned with their knowledge. I am the first to try to visit you in person. I brought back your record.'

Shermin smiled. 'We found it, in your craft.' Glad Fox wasn't present, he asked, 'What do you want here?'

'We are interested in your species.'

'You're some kind of anthropologist? Is that all you're doing here, checking us out? You didn't come to size up our military potential?'

'"Size up? Military potential?" Oh, I understand. No. Our only interest in your "military potential" is as it interrelates to the rest of your culture. I am interested in it, though. I am interested in all cultural aberrations.

'You see, you are a strange species, unlike any other we have discovered. And you would be surprised how many others there are, some intelligent, some savage, others who combine characteristics of both. You fall into the later category, though even there you are exceptional.'

'How many "others" are there?' Shermin asked him.

'Hundreds.'

'Oh.' Shermin swallowed. 'What do you do once you've made contact with another intelligence?'

'Some we make friends with and try to help. Others we ignore.'

'You're not afraid of the ones you ignore?'

'No. There is no reason to be. Generally they resolve their own fate in spectacular if sad fashion before they can become a danger to any peoples other than themselves.'

'Is that what you think's going to happen to us?'

'I am not sure. As I said, you are a strange species. There are many of my kind who think you are not worth the special effort it would take to help you survive. I confess that I was among them – until I came here myself. Shall I tell you what I find worth saving here? What I find beautiful and irreplaceable about you? Beautiful and contradictory? It is this: you are at your very best when things are at their worst.' He was piercing Shermin with his gaze and the advisor found himself trembling again under that relentless, challenging stare.

Jenny noted the position of the hands on the wall clock, glanced at the brightening sky outside. 'It's almost sun up, Mister Shermin. Let him go, please.'

'I can't. I told you. I'm not a decision maker. I'm just an overeducated flunky who does what he's told.'

'If he stays here and doesn't go with his friends, he'll die. Can't you understand that? He's dying now.'

Shermin inspected the visitor. 'You look okay to me. A little pale, maybe, but otherwise okay.'

The visitor smiled back at him. 'The change always comes from within. In less than one hour of yours I will be as dead as this form I have adopted.'

Shermin considered, and thought, and then he did something he'd just confessed to not being able to do: he decided.

If only he hadn't smiled. If only he'd expressed outrage, or had gotten mad, or had tried to break away and fight his way out. That's what Shermin told everyone later. It was that damn smile that had done it.

He rose suddenly. 'Both of you come with me.'

Jenny hesitated only momentarily, then took the starman by the hand and followed Shermin outside.

The sky to the east had gone from blue to pink. It was bright enough now to see without the aid of flashlights. The police cruisers had turned off their spots.

Shermin leaned over to whisper something to Jenny. She searched his face. 'You're serious, aren't you?'

He tried to shrug it off. 'Your friend said that ours is a society full of aberrations. Consider this one of mine. It'll make an interesting footnote in my journal.'

'Thank you. I don't know what to say. I—' She stood on tiptoes and kissed him hard before he could pull away. Not that he wanted to. The starman watched without comment. Then he too stepped forward and bussed the startled consultant.

'Uh, thanks,' Shermin told them, wiping his mouth.

He watched as they hurried through the milling state troopers and climbed into the Cadillac. Jenny Hayden slid behind the wheel. The car pulled out of the lot and started up the narrow road that led to the crater. The young sergeant from the cafe joined him.

'Not the right ones, huh?' He gazed at the dust the Eldorado was kicking up in its wake. 'They sure as hell fit the description. The car had Nevada plates, too.'

'Nah, close but no prize,' Shermin replied casually. 'Guy we're after's much older. I never did trust that report out of Vegas.' He removed his last cigar from a coat pocket and began to peel it slowly, lovingly. He was looking quite pleased with himself when the *whup-whup* of an approaching helicopter caused the sergeant and his fellow officers to look up. Shermin didn't. He knew who it was.

Fox was the first one out of the chopper. He sprinted for the cafe, moving with unexpected speed for a desk-bound bureaucrat. Halfway to the door, he spotted Shermin and the sergeant and changed course toward them. His eyes searched the interior of the patrol car, Shermin's face. Something told the security director that all hadn't gone according to plan. Maybe it was his advisor's grin.

'Where are they? What's happened to them? They still inside?' When Shermin didn't respond he turned to the state trooper. 'Sergeant, where are your prisoners?'

'Wrong ones,' the officer told him, sounding a mite puzzled. 'We let 'em go. What's all the fuss about?' Suddenly his gaze narrowed and he turned to look questioningly at Shermin.

You could see the thoughts racing through Fox's brain, lining up like magnets. He glanced a last time at Shermin before rushing to the cafe. He threw open the door and found himself staring at the night cook. He was the only one present.

'Hi,' said the man. 'I'm fixin' to close until six. That's when we open for breakfast.' He looked happy as he peered around the security director. 'Quite a crew you got out there. I expect they'll all be wanting to eat. There's still some cherry cobbler left. Say, what's this all ab—?'

Fox let the door slam behind him, cutting off the older man's query.

He strode up to Shermin until their belt buckles were practically touching, but the advisor didn't back away. 'You're finished, Shermin,' he said tightly. 'I'll have you eviscerated for this. You'll never work for another government agency or a company holding a government contract as long as you live.'

186

'Is that a promise?'

'Be as snide as you want. It's your last chance.'

'In that case, as much as I hate to resort to symbolism,' Shermin said calmly. He'd fired up his cigar while the security chief had been making his inspection of the cafe. Now he removed the brown bomber from his mouth and, with an inordinate amount of delight, blew a thick cloud of smoke straight into the taller man's face.

An occasional rumble of thunder could be heard as Jenny sent the Cadillac careening down the narrow, empty road, but no raindrops splattered the bug-stained windshield.

'There it is,' she whispered as a ridge of unnatural regularity came into view ahead. 'You don't seem excited.'

'I am conserving my strength,' he replied with a wan smile. 'I am very tired now, Jennyhayden.'

She smiled back encouragingly. 'Don't worry. We'll make it.'

She pulled to a stop in the deserted parking lot, led him up the first marked trail toward the crater rim. By the time they'd begun their descent he was having to lean on her for support.

Something in the sky growled, and this time it wasn't thunder.

'Got 'em!' The chopper's copilot was peering through the windshield of the big S-65, eyeing the ground.

Fox pressed between pilot and copilot, trying to see over the latter's shoulder. 'Where? Where?'

'Walking across the bottom of the crater, sir. The light's not good, but they're the only thing moving down there.'

Fox scanned the horizon. 'Where the hell are the gunships?' He hefted a pickup, spoke into it. 'Angel Command to Angel One. Where are you?'

'Don't worry, sir,' said the copilot. 'Where can they run to?'

Jenny stopped to look back the way they'd come. The rim of the crater was a stark black silhouette against the rapidly intensifying light. The faint singing sound was growing steadily louder.

'I hear something.'

187

The starman paused to listen. 'I have heard it before. Aircraft are coming.'

Even as they stared, four Cobra gunships suddenly appeared, barely clearing the crater ridge.

'What now?' Jenny asked him.

'Now? There is nothing more for us to do, Jennyhayden.' He tilted back his head and scanned the thickening clouds, but the sky was still devoid of promise.

The first chopper came in low and fast, its machine guns chewing up the sand in front of them. Warning bursts, Jenny thought wildly.

The starman stood murmuring next to her. Even his voice was growing faint, she noticed. 'No, no. This is all wrong. So wrong,' he murmured softly.

Another helicopter popped over the ridge, remained hovering back by the crater wall. An insistent voice reached them via amplifier. 'Mrs Hayden. This is George Fox of the National Security Agency. You and your companion must surrender immediately.'

The first chopper swung around and sprayed the sand and cinders a second time. The bullets landed very close.

'Last warning, Mrs Hayden,' the voice boomed. 'There can be no argument and no discussion. National security is in question here. I promise you that no one will be harmed, but you and your companion must surrender immediately or . . .'

'Jesus Christ,' gasped the helicopter pilot, speaking over Fox's ultimatum, 'what's that?'

It looked like a dust devil, but it was growing much too rapidly. Heretofor not so much as a light breeze had disturbed the floor of the crater. Now there was a dust devil moving toward the center of the basin and the two people standing there. A brisk wind sprang up seemingly from out of nowhere. Dust began to rise from the crater floor, obscuring everything from sight.

Fox was screaming into the mike. 'Take 'em out! That's an order. Take 'em out now!'

As he spoke the wind rose from a stiff breeze to gale force. Suddenly the chopper pilots were too busy fighting to stay airborne to worry about hitting a couple of tiny targets on the ground below. The helicopters bucked crazily in the sudden disturbance. As the wind rose outside, the barometer plunged.

Something came out of the bottom of the clouds. It was a ship, or rather, the underside of a ship. It was not quite as big as the Capitol building back in Washington, through whose quiet halls Fox had strode purposefully only a couple of days ago. Of course, it was only the bottom part of the ship. The rest was concealed by burgeoning stormclouds and the dust devils that were multiplying on the floor of the crater.

Jenny put her hands to her ears, wincing in sudden pain. She swallowed hard and the pain went away. It was just like descending a steep mountain road, she thought.

As she reacted to the abrupt drop in pressure, it began to snow. The white stuff fell out of the clouds that surrounded the great ship and began to accumulate on the cinders.

Suddenly they were bathed in red light, a soft ruby glow a hundred feet across. Instantly the wind ceased, though it continued to snow.

Outside the circle of red light the helicopters bucked madly as their pilots fought to cope with the storm that had assaulted them without warning. Fox yelled and threatened and demanded, but one by one the choppers were forced to retreat. The alternative, as the copilot of the S-65 attempted to explain to the apoplectic security director, was to be shaken to pieces or smashed against the crater wall.

Jenny had forgotten about the helicopters. She stood close to the starman in the beautifully quiet, red snowstorm, the big flakes falling gently all around them. Even her frosted breath was faintly red. Her expression was serene as she observed the starman's resurrection.

As soon as the light had touched him he'd seemed to straighten. Color had returned to his face, albeit red-tinged, and strength and confidence to his voice. He gazed at her solemnly and said the words she'd dreaded to hear, yet knew she must.

'I have to go now.'

'Take me with you.' How strange to say such a thing, she thought. Strange because it sounded so natural, because it was said so easily. Within her there was neither concern nor fear for the future.

An impossible future, which he realized even if she did not want to.

'I cannot.'

'Please.'

He glanced significantly upward. 'You would die there. As I would die here. Or worse, you would slowly suffocate from loneliness, deprived of the companionship of others of your own kind.'

'I don't think I'd care.'

'I care. I must go and you must stay. It is the way of things. Sometimes there are certain things experience cannot prepare us for, and I suspect this is one of them. That is as true for me as it is for you. Now, tell me again how to say good-bye.'

She shuddered slightly, and not from the cold. 'You kiss me and say that you love me.'

The starman remembered the movie. He put his arms around her and held her tight. Then he said, 'I love you.' How odd. Odd because it felt so natural, so normal, and was anything but.

'I'm never going to see you again, am I?' she asked him.

'It is extremely unlikely. No. I will not play a game with you. You will never see me again.'

She was crying now, the tears warm on her cheeks. He kissed the droplets away, then kissed her full on the lips.

'I love you.' She sobbed. 'That's crazy insane, isn't it? We're nothing alike.'

'That is where you are wrong. The body is nothing more than a shell, a frail envelope that contains the spirit. In spirit we are very much alike. Tell the baby about me. I believe there will come a time when he will be able to understand.'

'I will.'

He held her a moment longer. Then he stepped back and removed two things from the pocket of the windbreaker. One was the still unsigned check from the casino in Las

Vegas. The other was a small gray sphere about the size of a marble. The last gray sphere.

'These are for you.'

She took them both, stared at the gray sphere.

'What do I do with this? I've seen you use these, but I . . .'

'It is not for you,' he told her. 'It is for the child. When he is old enough to understand complex concepts, explain to him where it comes from. It is full of – imprints. Information. Other things you have no name for. He will take it and sleep with it and it will help him to mature properly. To realize his potential. Your potential.' He moved to kiss her a last time.

'Good-bye, Jennyhayden.' Then he turned and walked away from her, off into the red snow.

'Good-bye. Good-bye.' She clutched the sphere to her like a talisman and stared after him. He never looked back.

The red glow seemed to contract around him, becoming incredibly bright. Much later, when she'd had time to look back on it and consider, she couldn't have said if the light had swallowed him up or if he'd become part of it.

And then he was gone.

The red light began to fade. The snow stopped falling and the temperature rose. She had to swallow again as the pressure changed. The great ship began to recede skyward, vanishing into the cloud layer on the first step of its journey back to somewhere infinitely far away.

'Good-bye,' she whispered a last time. Off in the distance she could hear one of the helicopters hesitantly probing the crater rim. In a few minutes its pilot would discover that the powerful winds which had driven him and his colleagues away had disappeared as rapidly and mysteriously as they had materialized. Then they would come for her.

It didn't matter. Nothing mattered now.

No, that wasn't quite true. Something did matter, mattered very much. They were going to ask her questions, a lot of questions. She would answer them all, politely and at length, and eventually they would tire of hearing the same ones over and over again and then they would let her go home, back to Wisconsin.

But she wouldn't tell them the one thing they would find the most interesting. She wouldn't tell them because it was none of their business. It was a private matter.

She touched her belly lightly and rested her hand there, and by the time Fox's helicopter touched down nearby she was smiling.

THE END